The start of an expl(

C000097618

SAINT'S PASSAGE

Carwyn ap Bryn and Brigid Connor are two elemental vampires finding the lost, righting wrongs, and searching for meaning in the endless stretch of immortality they've been granted.

And trying not to blow things up, but that might be more aspirational.

Everyone said that Lupe Martínez was a good kid. She listened to her mom, she helped at the homeless shelter, she got good grades, and she had a bright future ahead of her.

Until she disappeared.

Now no one knows what to think. The police are sure she ran away; her mother is sure she didn't. Days have passed and no one knows what to do until her family priest suggests they call in an old friend.

A *very* old friend.

Saint's Passage is the first book in the paranormal mystery series Elemental Covenant by Elizabeth Hunter, *USA Today* best-selling author of the Elemental Legacy series, the Glimmer Lake Series, and the Irin Chronicles.

We get Carwyn's optimism and wit with Brigid's fiery personality. Their banter is on point.

I love where this new series is going and I can't wait to read more.

Is it too cheesy to call this an explosive new series? Because, well...as it turns out, when you have a fire *and* an earth elemental vampire teaming up to solve a mystery, things can get...rocky.

SAINT'S PASSAGE

ELEMENTAL COVENANT BOOK ONE

ELIZABETH HUNTER

For everyone who has made it this far

PROLOGUE

María Guadalupe Martínez Estrada stared up at the painting of Christ with children climbing up his knees and playing with the ends of his robes. She glanced at the sputtering flames of the prayer candles beneath the painting and wondered what each candle represented.

A sick child? An unexpected pregnancy? An angry parent?

It was Lupe's favorite place to wait in Saint Peter's church when she was killing time before youth-group duties. Most of the time, this chapel was empty and she could check her phone or read a book in peace.

Tonight her phone battery was dangerously low, so she stared at the painting. There were children of every color and various ages. Some had fine clothes, but most had shirts that were worn or scuffed on the edges.

A plaque at the bottom of the painting bore the words "LET THE LITTLE CHILDREN COME TO ME, AND DO NOT HINDER THEM. FOR THE KINGDOM OF HEAVEN BELONGS TO SUCH AS THESE."

It was a nice idea. A good goal, Lupe thought. It wasn't reality. In the middle of Los Angeles—the "city of angels"—it was more an ironic joke than anything else.

She was waiting by the painting while Father Anthony told the new kids what they'd be doing that night and what they might expect at the rescue mission. Saint Peter's youth group helped out serving meals and cleaning rooms one night a week for the family quarters at the mission while some of the older kids like Lupe set up the warming center when temperatures dropped and then went out in "street teams" to talk to families that might need help.

Focus on the kids, Father Anthony always said. *We can't help everyone every night, so we focus on the most vulnerable. Get those kids indoors.*

People thought it didn't get cold in LA. That was bullshit. It was January, and they'd had nearly a week of almost freezing temperatures. That might not seem like much for someone from a place that snowed, but when you lived on the street, the cold was enough to keep you miserable at night, especially if you were a little kid.

"Hey, Lupe."

She turned to see Joshua Gomez enter the chapel.

"Hey." She looked back to the painting, her eyes fixed on the lit candles. Josh would want to talk. He always wanted to talk. Mostly about himself. Maybe she could convince him she was praying.

"Did you see how many freshmen came tonight?" He sat next to her. "I guess my talk last Sunday must have motivated them, huh?"

So no luck on the praying thing. "Yeah, probably." More

likely it had to do with report cards coming out and college-bound kids realizing they needed volunteer hours if they wanted to be eligible for the good scholarships, but she didn't mention that. She glanced back and saw a middle-aged priest leading a group of younger teens from the youth-group meeting room. "Looks like we're ready to go."

"Good." Josh stood when Lupe did. "So... you want to be on the street team with me tonight?"

Lupe glanced toward the meeting room. Teaming up with Josh wasn't exactly in her plan, but she didn't know how to turn him down without him getting suspicious. "Um... Yeah, I guess. I might have to stick close to the mission though. I kinda had that thing last week with the guy from Streets Alive, remember?"

Josh shrugged. "That dude? He won't bother you if you're with me."

"Uh-huh." Lupe hooked her backpack over her shoulder and headed toward the foyer of the church.

That's what I'm afraid of.

———

LUPE STUFFED her hands in the pockets of her thickest jacket, keeping her bright blue rescue-mission shirt visible as she walked through the park with Josh and Mika Walker, one of the other senior girls. Mika and Josh were debating the merits of dorm life at UCLA and USC, which was where Mika wanted to attend.

And Lupe? Well, college was a little more complicated for her.

She kept her eyes out for any small faces peeking from tents or the backs of cars parked in the scattered parking spaces. The mission had beds open tonight in the family wing.

"...don't you think, Lupe?"

She snapped to attention at the sound of her name, turning to Mika and Josh. "Huh?"

"I was saying that talking about which college dorms are nicer seems a little tone-deaf when we're trying to help homeless families." Mika kept her voice low and glanced at Josh. "Don't you think?"

"Yeah. I mean..." Lupe kept hearing Daniel's snide remarks in the back of her head.

Privileged rich kids with a hero complex.

Do-gooders without a clue.

Blue-shirts looking for social justice points.

"I think we should focus on seeing if there are any kids our age," she said. "I'm not seeing anyone that looks like they're with a family. I haven't seen any littles, have you?"

"No." Mika smiled a little. "Which is good. I'm with you. Let's see if we can find anyone a little older."

Kids their age were probably the trickiest to deal with and often the most resistant to help. Any kid under eighteen knew they could go back into the system, which was how many of them had wound up on the streets in the first place. So most kids they talked to—even those obviously younger—said they were eighteen.

And technically, kids over eighteen needed to go to the single men or single women's housing, which wasn't where the kids from Saint Peter's worked. And it wasn't where a vulnerable teen should be either.

"Come on," Lupe said, tugging Josh's sleeve. "We can ask Tonya if she's seen anyone new."

Tonya was one of the activists in charge of Streets Alive, the homeless advocacy group that regularly worked downtown. They had a big converted van that drove around to all the encampments and were connected with all the city services and charities. Tonya was an older woman, and she had a soft spot for teen girls, often defying the people from Social Services who tried to find out their identities and ages.

"If the system had been safe, they wouldn't have left."

That's what Tonya usually said about her girls, and it had stuck with Lupe. She knew, better than her friends did, that just because something was legal, it wasn't necessarily right. And just because something was illegal, it wasn't necessarily wrong.

Lupe spotted Daniel immediately when they walked around the public bathroom and saw Tonya set up in the front parking lot. She was standing in front, talking to a group of women, and had two teen girls with her handing out brown paper bags with sandwiches. Daniel was standing at the back of the van, talking and passing out bulky blankets wrapped in plastic.

Thick, dark hair fell to his shoulders, and his light brown complexion was tanned from spending most of his days outdoors. His mouth was set in a serious line that didn't shift an inch when he caught sight of Lupe.

She glanced at him but looked away quickly. How old was he? He'd never said. *Too old,* her mother would say.

It didn't matter; that wasn't why she needed to talk to him. It wasn't like that.

Keep telling yourself that.

Lupe knew she was flirting with a crush; she also knew Daniel would sneer at the word. And the idea. He wasn't working on the streets to meet a naive girl from Huntington Park.

She hiked her backpack on her shoulder and hung back as Josh and Mika approached Tonya, who was setting up chairs and a portable fireplace where people could get warm. Lupe stayed at the edge of the gathering crowd and waited for his voice.

"I told you not to come with your little friends."

She glanced over her shoulder, then quickly moved her eyes forward. "Father Anthony doesn't let us wander around by ourselves at night. Groups of two or three only."

"Am I gonna have to stage an argument with you again?"

Lupe huffed. She was kind of sick of Daniel's cloak-and-dagger silliness. She didn't understand why everything had to be so secret. "Just tell me what the plan is. My mom isn't working tomorrow night, so I'm gonna have to—"

"It's not tomorrow night, it's tonight."

She turned, not caring if anyone noticed them. "What? That wasn't what we talked about."

"Plans had to change. Deal with it." Daniel couldn't seem to meet her eyes. "I got the car and the money tonight. You think there's time to hang out and wait?"

Lupe didn't know what to say. "I need more time" seemed selfish. "I don't have anything ready."

Daniel stepped closer to her, and in a place that mostly smelled like urine and human sweat, he smelled clean, masculine, and safe. "You don't have to have stuff ready, Lupe. You have to *be* ready." His dark eyes met hers. "Are you?"

She glanced at Mika and Josh, then back to Daniel. "Okay, tell me what to do. Right now, while they're talking to Tonya."

Daniel leaned down and began to whisper in her ear.

By the time Mika and Josh turned around, Lupe Martínez was gone.

CHAPTER ONE

New York City, NY
One week later

B rigid Connor glanced to her right and saw the shadow of a mountain at her shoulder. "Are you sure we know what we're doing here?"

The mountain looked down. "Do we ever?"

Brigid shrugged. "Fair point."

"Just give us your stuff and you can go," the scrawny human holding the gun said.

The two men at the end of the alley were very convinced that the two people in evening wear whom they'd taken for tourists were clueless and would hand over their wallets now that they'd been cornered by "menacing" humans. The men had heard the heavy accents, seen the two strangers looking at a map of downtown. An honest-to-goodness map! Who used a map these days?

Had to be stupid foreign tourists.

"This dress doesn't have a single place to carry a gun," Brigid said. "Can't believe I didn't think of that."

"We're going to a gallery opening." The mountain, also known as her mate, Carwyn, spoke casually. "Admittedly, the New York art scene has been described as murderous, but who wouldn't assume that was a metaphor?"

The men exchanged glances. The foreigners in the evening clothes didn't seem worried.

"We said" —the stockier human stepped forward and raised his firearm— "hand over your stuff. Do that and nobody gets hurt."

Brigid saw the dull black barrel the human pointed at her and cocked her head. "Oh hello, my pretty. Is that a Kimber nine millimeter? That's a step up from the usual, isn't it? Carwyn, look at this."

Carwyn was starting to squirm in the dress clothes he'd been forced to don for the evening. "I've never had your penchant for firearms, darling girl. Can't tell one from the other. Bang, bang, ow. That's roughly the extent of my firearms acumen."

"I'm just sayin'…" What was she thinking? They were wasting time. She pulled her gaze from the lovely pistol and looked at the man holding the gun on her. "Listen, before I give you my purse, can I grab my lighter from the pocket?" She laid her Irish accent on thick. "See, it was me own dear da's, and he's passed and it's the last thing I have of his. It's not dear or anything of the sort, but if you could just—"

"Fine!" The robber relented, no doubt just a little nervous that the extremely large man behind her didn't seem anxious in the least and was inching closer as every moment passed.

Carwyn kicked at the asphalt. "Brigid, my love."

"Yes, dear?" Brigid made a show of looking through her small purse.

"One thing I've noticed about these New York alleys? They really have a lot of potholes."

"Is that so?" Her fingers closed around the lighter. "All the way down to the mud? Is that what yer saying?"

The second man was getting nervous. "Will you two shut up and hand over—"

"Found my lighter." Brigid's fingers closed around the cool metal.

"About time."

At once, Brigid dropped her purse and flicked the lighter open as Carwyn fell to the ground, one arm shooting out to catch her handbag as the other hand pushed into the pothole where he'd been kicking asphalt.

Brigid braced herself for the quick jolt as Carwyn's elemental power hit the earth beneath her feet. It threw both the humans holding guns off-balance. She hit the lighter and caught the flame in her hand, feeding it until it she held twin balls of fire.

"Guns are less noticeable in this country" —she advanced on the two humans and smiled, letting her fangs drop— "but they're not the only weapon I have."

The two men started screaming. They threw their guns at Brigid, who tossed the amber-gold fireball in the air and caught the Kimber.

"Come to me, my pretty." She cooed at the abused nine millimeter, letting the other gun clatter to the ground. "Carwyn?"

"One more." He grunted and the ground rolled again.

The two men curled into themselves as Brigid flung the

other fireball toward them, letting the flames spread and dissipate close enough to burn their eyebrows but not harm them any more than that.

Carwyn rose, one hand filthy with mud and grime, the other holding the sparkly purse she'd borrowed for the evening.

"There you go." He glanced at the gun. "And look at that. Your new pistol might just fit."

"What a lad you are." Brigid rose on her toes and kissed him. "Smart move, marrying you." She pointed her chin at the two humans. "What shall we do with these two?"

"We're going to be late as it is, and I've got to find some place to clean up a bit." He looked down. "It's a good thing this suit is dark grey."

"The sleeve is a bit tragic, but I doubt anyone will notice." Brigid looked at the trembling balls of human at the end of the alley, then at the dumpster next to Carwyn. "Maybe just put them in the skip for a bit."

Carwyn nodded, walked over, and picked up one curled human as if he were a duffel bag, tossing him in the dumpster before he added the other. He snarled at the two men, baring long, thick fangs that gleamed in the streetlights.

"If you want to live," he growled in a menacing voice, "don't even think about moving."

Brigid smelled the distinct odor of fresh urine in the dumpster.

Good man. That should keep the two away from any other tourists until they could nab the attention of the Gardaí.

Check that, NYPD. They weren't in Dublin anymore.

Brigid slid the compact nine millimeter into her purse.

"Look at that. It does fit. Lovely. I'll have to ask Chloe where she got this handbag."

"You know…" Carwyn wrinkled his nose. "We smell like we've been playing in downtown Manhattan alleys."

"Imagine that." She nudged him toward the end of the alley that led to the street. "We'll ask the driver to keep the windows down on the way there. Maybe they won't notice."

———

THE DRIVER WAS on his phone, no doubt trying to find his passengers, when they met him on Wooster Street.

"Hey!" His cheery face reminded Brigid to smile and put her fangs away.

Don't scare the nice humans.

"Hello." She quickly heated her skin and reached out to shake his hand. "Sorry, someone thought it would be a lovely idea for a walk before the gallery opening, and then we found ourselves a bit lost."

"No worries. We have a long drive in front of us. I just want to make sure we get there in time."

"Do we?" Brigid shot Carwyn a look. "Quite a drive, is it?"

Carwyn's vivid blue eyes were all innocence. "Didn't I tell you?"

Brigid tossed her purse in the luxurious black sedan and slid into the back seat, pushing back her annoyance while she waited for Carwyn to finish speaking to the driver. She scooted all the way across the plush bench and pressed herself against the far door, her fingers sparking against the power window lever before she leaned away.

Fuck. New cars and fire vampires didn't get along. Fire

13

vampires and any electronics tended not to get along. It was damned inconvenient and more than a little limiting in the twenty-first century.

Humans. Constantly determined to make life more complicated.

It would have been easy for Brigid to say that her pessimistic attitude toward humanity was shaped by her transformation into a vampire over ten years before, but that wasn't strictly true. She'd been pessimistic about humanity since she was a child.

Brigid had always felt more at home with monsters.

She glanced at her husband standing outside the door, gesturing dramatically and joking with the human driver as he gave directions to their destination.

Extroverts. Why had she married one again?

Despite being roughly the size of a small boulder, Carwyn ap Bryn—earth vampire, former Catholic priest, her blood mate, and regrettable extrovert—eased into the sedan gracefully, sliding his fingers down the back of her bare arm until he could link their hands. Brigid's fangs lengthened in reaction.

"What did you get me into?"

He turned to her and grinned, his smile lighting up the shadowed seat compartment. His head brushed the roof, and his red hair appeared deep auburn in the darkness. "It'll be good craic. Promise."

"A hundred humans stuffed in a gallery looking at paintings doesn't sound like good craic. Not unless it's some kind of spontaneous buffet you haven't told me about."

He laughed. "Darling, bloodthirsty girl." He quickly

kissed the back of her hand before he released it and pointed to the side of the car. "Seat belt."

The corner of Brigid's mouth turned up in a sneer. "Don't be daft."

Carwyn glanced at the human driver, who had opened the door. "Safety first."

They were both immortal vampires whose bodies could repair themselves from anything save beheading or fire. Brigid wasn't worried about a rollover in downtown Manhattan.

Brigid muttered, "Are you questioning my judgment?"

Carwyn looked at the driver. Back to Brigid. "I believe it's the law in the state of New York."

"If that's how you want to play." Brigid reached for the irritating buckle to click it in the latch before she nodded at Carwyn's side. "Now it's your turn."

Amusement flared in his eyes. He reached over, grabbed the seat belt, and pulled it over his shoulder, holding the buckle near his waist.

Brigid batted her eyelashes. "Oh, my love, I don't think *holding* the belt is sufficient. What if we were to be involved in a dangerous *motor vehicle accident*?" She spoke slowly and allowed her voice to rise so the driver could hear her.

The driver glanced in the rearview mirror. "Yes, sir, I'm going to need both of you to buckle up."

"Right." Carwyn's eyes narrowed and he turned back to Brigid, speaking in Irish so the driver couldn't understand. "You're a right vicious little thing. You want me to cut off circulation to my balls?"

"I think your balls are safe." Brigid knew the average human seat belt barely fit across Carwyn's broad frame, but it did fit. Barely. She reached for a bottle of water tucked in the back pocket of the car.

Carwyn was still clutching the safety buckle in his massive fist. "I'm just saying" —he continued in English— "if my balls are safe, I imagine the rest of me will be too."

Brigid nearly spat out the water she'd been about to swallow when she saw the look on their poor driver's face. "You have such a way with words."

He leaned closer to her, teasing. "You know I'm right."

"About your balls?"

"And other things."

Their car could probably fly off a cliff and her husband would manage to extricate both of them and weather the landing without a scratch.

"Think of our poor driver whose ears you've just violated." Brigid nodded at the human in the dark uniform. "If his car were stopped, he could be held liable for any passengers not wearing a safety belt properly. Don't be a scofflaw, Carwyn."

"A scofflaw?" He was barely containing his laugh.

The driver bravely piped up. "Sir, I really do need you to wear a safety belt. Thank you."

Brigid cocked her head and shrugged. "You heard the man."

The corner of Carwyn's lip twitched. "So thoughtful." He pulled the safety belt across his lap as the car began to move. "Really just..." He grunted and fought to click the latch near his hip. "...considerate. So considerate."

"People say that about me all the time." Brigid watched him yank the belt. "They remark on it constantly."

"My thoughtful, tenderhearted" —he huffed as he struggled— "angel of a wife."

"I'm so glad you appreciate me." She reached over and patted his knee. "You're welcome."

Eventually Carwyn battled with the belt long enough that they heard a satisfying *click*. "There. Happy?"

"With you? Always."

Carwyn grumbled. "Stop being sweet when I'm irritated with you."

Brigid—eager to make the minutes pass swiftly—closed her eyes, leaned her head against his shoulder, and attempted to drift. "Tell me again why we're going to this thing."

Carwyn's hand came up to play in the short crop of her thick sable hair. "We're going to honor the invitation of a former client who invited us to a significant life milestone. It's important."

"We're intruding."

"She invited us. She wants us to be there."

But why? Brigid wanted to know and she didn't. "How long will the drive take?"

"Two hours."

"Fuck *me*." She groaned. "Two hours?"

"Really can't do that in a hired car like this," Carwyn said quietly. "Even if there was a divider, it seems rude. If you're determined though, I'd risk it to escape this safety belt."

She couldn't help the laugh that bubbled up. "Obnoxious man."

Adriana Guzman had been a bright and talented seventeen-year-old art student when she disappeared without a trace two and a half years before. Police had written off her case, assuming she'd run away with a boyfriend, but Adriana's mother had known her daughter wouldn't do anything of the sort.

So she'd called a newspaper, the newspaper had called a reporter on the West Coast who'd investigated similar cases, and that news had eventually filtered up to Brigid, who had been taking some time away from her security duties to the vampire lord of Dublin. She and Carwyn had been free-lancing with various allies of her boss around the globe and stretching her skills a bit.

They'd found Adriana in a matter of weeks, but her case had been the first link in a long chain that eventually led to the Sokolov crime family, which was an ongoing matter that crossed numerous international vampire jurisdictions.

In short, it was tricky and Brigid was still working on it.

In the years since her kidnapping, the young woman had attempted to reclaim her life and leave the scars of her abduction in the past.

And though Brigid knew Adriana had moved on, gradu-ated high school, and been accepted to an extremely presti-gious art program, the image Brigid had in her mind was a hurt girl, confused and angry, who reminded Brigid a little too much of herself.

She concentrated on the feel of Carwyn's fingers sliding along her nape.

Though she was a predator now, she'd been a victim. She hated anything that reminded her of that. "Is she the only artist presenting?"

"No," Carwyn said. "I spoke to her mother. This is for the whole freshman class, keeping in mind this school only accepts around fifteen painting students each year."

"And Adriana was one of them?" Brigid couldn't help but be impressed. She hadn't been a keen student. She'd been more interested in police tactics, criminology, and weapons, much to her foster parents' dismay. "I still don't understand why she wants us there." She kept her voice low. "We only knew her during a horrible part of her life."

Carwyn pressed his lips together. "You'll understand when we get there. Just keep an open mind."

CHAPTER TWO

B rigid was still wondering why she needed an open mind when they pulled into the parking lot of the student gallery, which was lit up and glowing from a distance.

Judging by the number of luxury cars in the parking lot and the news van near the entrance, this wasn't anything like a high school talent show.

"Do you see?" Brigid nodded at the van as they made their way inside.

Carwyn clutched her hand. "Cameras. We'll have to keep an eye out." Every year technology like facial recognition made life harder for the immortal.

"Murphy needs to get cracking on those jammers." Brigid's boss, Patrick Murphy, was a technical wizard as well as being a water vampire and immortal lord of Dublin. He was working on a portable device that would disable digital cameras and phones.

Carwyn muttered something Brigid couldn't hear.

"What's that?"

"Just wondering if they've ordered food for this do."

That wasn't what he'd said, but she ignored the lie. He'd probably muttered something about Murphy. Her husband and her boss could push each other's buttons, and Brigid tried to stay out of it.

Too much testosterone if she had to guess. Both were hardheaded and high-handed. While Carwyn tried to disguise his pushiness with a jovial demeanor, he still got his way more often than not. Murphy was a bit more directly ruthless.

"Fuck," Brigid muttered as the gallery came into view. "Far too many people."

"Jaysus, it's heaving, isn't it?" He looked down. "Buffet jokes aside, you fed tonight, didn't you?"

"When I woke up." And she didn't keep to the animal-only diet her husband prescribed to. There were donors at the vampire club in the Bowery near their guest room, and she was more than happy to pay for their services. Carwyn was over a thousand years old and could get by on a meal of deer blood every few weeks. Brigid was far younger.

As they entered the foyer of the crowded gallery, the scent of humanity hit her in all its sweaty, perfumed, sprayed, and primped glory. The salt-and-copper smell of human blood surrounded her, and Brigid knew her fangs had fallen without a second thought.

Just another reason not to smile.

Carwyn had paused in the foyer and was staring at her.

She glanced up. "What?"

"You look lush, wife." His bright blue eyes glowed with appreciation, set off by his uncharacteristically formal grey suit. The only splash of color was the vivid blue shirt he wore open at the collar. "Like a pixie with an anger management problem."

"You say the sweetest things." She looked down at the wine-colored dress that clung to her body. "I borrowed it from Tenzin. Do you know all her clothes have pockets to keep knives in?"

"I don't find that surprising. Still, looks better on you."

"You might be biased." She squeezed his hand. "Come on. Let's go find Adriana."

———

FINDING THE GIRL WAS EASY; speaking to her was not, primarily because the young woman appeared to be in the center of a mob of admirers. Carwyn and Brigid could only wave from a distance. While Carwyn went to look for Mrs. Guzman, Brigid worked her way through the art gallery until she reached a round room that she instinctively knew contained Adriana's paintings.

There was a bristling energy bordering on chaos that marked her work, as if the paintings themselves wanted to escape their canvases and explode over the walls. Vivid, luxurious scenes of what Brigid guessed was the Dominican Republic, where Adriana was born, along with street scenes almost too crowded with life, grit, and graffiti.

On the far wall, the unquestioned star of the show, was a series of self-portraits that nearly knocked Brigid over with their raw vulnerability.

On the far left was the wounded girl that Brigid remembered. Next to her, a raging hellion, screaming at the world with tears in her eyes, tangled hair, and gritted teeth. The center canvas stopped Brigid in her tracks.

In it, Adriana's long hair had been shaved close to the scalp—with bleeding cuts and angry scrapes—and everywhere in the canvas around her, fire filled the space. It caressed the girl's shoulders and whispered in her ears.

With one glance at the painful image, Brigid was thrown back in time.

Darkness. Fire. A twisting ache in her gut and a burning in her throat.

Burning. Everything was burning.

The smell of smoke filled her nose, and the fire rippled along her skin, soothing and scorching at the same time.

Brigid forced herself to see through the wash of memories. The next canvas was cooler, and instead of fire filling the space around her, there was color. Washes of indistinct color with no shape or sense, filling all the space the fire had burned away. The girl in the center of the canvas had her eyes closed. Maybe she was dreaming. Maybe she was floating in a sea of color. But the creases around her eyes were smooth again. The cuts and scrapes were healed. The face was softer.

The final canvas brought tears to Brigid's eyes. The eyes were open, soft and welcoming to the world. Full of cautious hope. In the space surrounding the hope, images of flowers and front stoops, vines curling around broken doors, binding them and covering them with verdant life.

"Do you like it?"

Brigid glanced over to see Adriana Guzman, her hair clipped in short tousled waves that hid her eyes. She was standing next to Brigid, watching her examine the paintings.

"It's brilliant." Brigid reached over, careful to warm her

hand, and squeezed the young woman's arm quickly before she dropped it. "It's feckin' brilliant. Well done."

"I remember the fire." Adriana frowned a little. "That chemical fire in the factory that night."

Chemical... Oh right. "Yes, the chemical fire." Brigid remembered the very short screams of some very bad men. The fire department had believed their story. Mostly.

Adriana continued. "I remember thinking that it was almost as if it followed you. Like it had a mind of its own. It flared up and then it was gone so quickly, and they were all gone."

It did follow me. And I burned every one of those evil bastards who hurt you.

"Fire, you know..." Brigid stared at the middle painting and felt her amnis ripple under her skin. It was the immortal energy that animated her and kept her alive; it was also the tie between her mind, her body, and the element she was learning to command. "Fire is a curious thing."

"I used to dream about the flames just..." Adriana turned her hand in a circular motion. "...rolling over me, you know? Taking me with them. And I'd just be gone."

"Fuck no! What a waste that would have been." Brigid looked around the room. "Yer so bloody talented—I'd give my right arm to be able to make anything this grand." Thoughts of craving oblivion were hardly new to Brigid, so the confession didn't surprise her, but she *was* surprised by how violently her mind revolted at the thought.

Adriana's cautious face broke into a wide smile. "Thanks. And thanks for coming tonight. I really wanted you to see..." She looked around the room. "Just... more than what you saw before, I guess."

"...when life breaks, you pick up the pieces and keep moving. Otherwise you stay broken. And instead of being a survivor, you're always a victim."

"Thank you for inviting us." Brigid looked around for Carwyn's tall profile. "Fair warning, my man's likely to eat all the fancy food if you've left anything out."

"My mom's catering company did the spread tonight, so I think she probably took Carwyn into account."

"Good thinking." Brigid nudged Adriana toward her family. "Tell me a bit about this school then. Hope yer not paying too much, 'cause yer already fucking good."

Adriana just laughed.

———

BRIGID LEANED against Carwyn in the back of the car. They'd both completely forgotten about safety belts. Thankfully, so had their driver.

"You were right," she said. "It's good we came."

"I know." His hand played with her knuckles. "You're good at protecting people, Brigid."

She kept her eyes closed and luxuriated in his quiet attention. "That's my job."

"You protect powerful people."

"Powerful people have powerful enemies."

"And sometimes ordinary people have powerful enemies too."

She frowned and opened her eyes, looking over her shoulder. "What are you getting at?"

"I've been thinking... we shouldn't go back to Dublin."

Carwyn drummed his fingers on his knee. "I think you should quit your job."

CHAPTER THREE

The Dancing Bear was a human bar in the theater district with a high tolerance for vampires. At least that was the impression Carwyn had when they first entered the cozy pub with red velvet booths, heavy green drapes, and theater-themed art on the walls.

It was a carnival of odd characters, and if Carwyn had been younger, he would have been hard-pressed to pick out his own kind among the kaleidoscope of humanity on display at two in the morning. There were humans in Goth makeup and vampires in period clothing. There were even humans and vampires who'd made body paint a feature of their evening couture.

The Dancing Bear was a bit of everything that made up New York, which meant a bit of everything in the world. In other words, it was an absolute delight and Carwyn's new favorite place to hang out.

Plus there was no mistaking the vampire behind the bar.

"Gavin." Carwyn leaned on the scarred stretch of oak. "Not your usual type of place."

Gavin Wallace was the owner of dozens of vampire clubs and restaurants around the globe, all of which were neutral territory for their kind. There was no feeding allowed, except from designated donors, and absolutely no violence. Usually Gavin's places felt subdued and serious.

The Dancing Bear?

Gavin set a short glass in front of Carwyn and filled it halfway with clear gold whisky. "You'll be honored to know that I bought it for Chloe but I named it after you."

Carwyn threw his head back and laughed. "I like you more since you met her."

The corner of Gavin's mouth turned up. "I like you more since I met her, as well."

Gavin, like so many of their kind, had fallen for an extraordinary human. Chloe was a dancer, a budding choreographer, and an old friend who was currently sitting with Carwyn's wife and an even older friend who was playing host to them while they were in the city.

"How long are you in New York?" Gavin asked, sipping his own drink as Carwyn lifted his. "Sláinte." He clinked Carwyn's glass. "Your business is finished, isn't it? You catching a slow boat back to Dublin soon?"

"Not if I can convince that one to quit her job." Carwyn nodded toward the booth where Brigid, Chloe, and their friend Tenzin were sharing a bottle of wine.

Gavin raised a curious eyebrow. "I didn't know Brigid was looking for a change."

"She's not. I am." Carwyn sipped his scotch. "She's outgrown him."

"Murphy?" Gavin shrugged. "Everyone knows that one of the reasons Ireland is so stable is that Brigid Fucking

Connor will incinerate anyone who irritates Patrick Murphy."

"Well, that's not precisely true. I irritate Murphy regularly, and she only occasionally tries to incinerate me."

Gavin smirked. "Still. It's allowed a flourishing vampire tech industry for the first time in history. You want to risk that?"

"Murphy would be risking nothing. The connection is still there. I still have family there. The security office she's established isn't moving, and it operates independent of her. Why do you think we're gone so much as it is?"

"Because you hate your wife's boss?"

The corner of Carwyn's lip curled up. "He's just so..."

"Polite."

"Fucking *yes*." Carwyn slammed a hand on the bar. "A proper, polite dandy these days. The only time I like the man is when I'm throwing him around a room or we're knocking seven shades of shite out of each other."

Gavin smiled as he sipped his drink. "You sound quite Irish these days."

"Don't remind me." He was far from his birthplace in South Wales and even farther from his last parish in North Wales where Welsh was the common tongue and life was far more subdued.

"I'm not craving quiet." He glanced around the bar. "I wouldn't be in this place if I was. I'm just craving... more. Something more meaningful than making sure rich, powerful vampires stay rich and powerful."

Gavin leaned against the bar. "Aren't you a rich, powerful vampire?"

"Please. I was a man of the cloth for centuries. The

rumors of my wealth are greatly exaggerated." They weren't, but Carwyn also had a massive clan to support. He had ten vampire offspring, all their children, and assorted relatives around the world. It gave him great influence and great obligations, all at the same time.

Gavin nodded at Brigid in the corner booth. "I'm not the one you need to convince, Father. Sounds like you need to be taking your arguments elsewhere."

Carwyn cut Gavin slack on referring to him by his old title since the barman had known him since long before he left the priesthood. He grabbed the bottle of scotch, refilled his glass, and walked to the table, dodging a pirate in Rollerblades on his way there.

Definitely hard to spot the vampires in this place.

He reached the table and slid into the booth next to Chloe before any of the women could speak.

"You are so large" —Tenzin narrowed her eyes at him— "and yet irritatingly quiet." She looked like a small East Asian woman who could have been anywhere between sixteen and thirty. In reality, she was a multimillennial-old wind vampire from prehistoric Mongolia, daughter of immortal royalty, and occasionally an assassin.

Carwyn's wife adored Tenzin and wanted to be her when she grew up, which was more than a little terrifying.

"Tenzin." Carwyn leaned across the table. "I think Brigid should quit her job with Murphy and work for herself. What do you think?"

Brigid glared at him.

Tenzin said, "I have never willingly worked for another vampire who wasn't my sire, so yes. Brigid should stop working for Murphy."

Chloe raised her hand. "Uh, not everyone wants to be their own boss. Just saying. Brigid, you said you enjoy working for Murphy."

"Well, I—"

"If she enjoys it, she shouldn't quit." Tenzin sipped her wine. "That would be illogical."

"But Brigid is independent by nature," Carwyn said. "It's part of what makes her such an excellent investigator."

Chloe said, "Weren't you, like, a priest for ages and ages? You weren't your own boss then."

Chloe Reardon was Gavin's partner, a vibrant woman with medium-brown skin and delightful curls that sprang wild all over her head. Normally Chloe enchanted Carwyn. Tonight she wasn't being much help.

"Church hierarchy and vampire hierarchy are completely different things," he said. "Whose side are you on?"

Chloe pointed at Brigid. "Hers. In whatever decision she makes as long as it's a healthy choice for her."

Carwyn muttered, "Kiss-up."

Tenzin leaned forward. "I should tell you Carwyn was a priest, but he was very bad at being obedient to his church masters."

"Thank you, Tenzin."

Chloe frowned. "Was that a compliment?"

Brigid raised her hand. "Would you like to know what I want?"

"Absolutely," Chloe said.

Carwyn and Tenzin exchanged a glance.

"Of course," Carwyn said dutifully.

Tenzin said, "I suppose."

"Yeah, you suppose," Brigid muttered. "It's not like it's my own life or anything."

Tenzin pointed at Carwyn. "But it's also his life."

"I know that, Tenzin. I married the fecker."

Tenzin looked at Carwyn, then back to Brigid. "If you're trying to make us respect your judgment, that might not be the thing to bring up."

"Oi!"

"I think..." Brigid raised her voice. "That I don't want to make this decision by committee. And I don't want to make this decision right now." She looked at Carwyn. "You brought this up in the car three hours ago and expected me to just jump for joy and say 'Absolutely, you brilliant man, we should do whatever you want,' and it's not that simple, Carwyn. It's not." Brigid finished her wine, set the glass down, and stood up. "I'm going for a pee. Who's coming with me?"

"You don't need to pee," Tenzin said.

"No, I really just want to move around and look at myself in the mirror to make sure my makeup isn't smeared to hell the way I'm fairly sure it is."

Chloe nudged Carwyn. "I'll go with you. And I'm human, so I do actually have to pee."

Brigid and Chloe departed for the female bonding ritual in the bar bathroom, leaving Carwyn and Tenzin alone at the table.

Tenzin stared at him. "Why do you really want her to quit?"

"I don't think she's happy."

"She says she is."

"And Ben never says he's happy, but you know he's really not?"

Tenzin had recently begun a relationship—an *actual*

romantic relationship—with Ben Vecchio, a young vampire who was also the son of one of Carwyn's oldest friends. It was an odd dynamic, but that was far from unusual in the immortal world. The fact that Tenzin had found companionship with anyone was a minor miracle in Carwyn's eyes. She wasn't the most well-adjusted vampire.

Tenzin said, "You're right. Ben is still quite human in that sense."

"Humans and vampires lie to themselves regularly," Carwyn said. "I know she's probably not going to jump at the change, but I want to put the idea in her mind. I think she stays with Murphy because he gave her a chance when she needed one, but obligation is a horrible reason to stay on in an organization. I did it too long with the church."

Tenzin nodded. "I will agree with you on that."

"Plus Brigid and I could be doing something more important than playing bodyguard for the rich and powerful. Murphy likes having her there—she adds to his reputation—but he doesn't *need* her. Not like other people do."

Tenzin glanced toward the corner where the women's bathrooms were, then back to Carwyn. "You're talking about finding people. Like Ben and I find treasure."

"I mean finding people." He finished his drink and leaned forward. "Returning them to their families. Helping them start new lives. Putting them on a safe path, whatever that means for them. Brigid couldn't rescue herself when she was a child. But there are other ways to slay our dragons. I want her to know that."

"Why not stay as you've been doing?" she asked. "She technically works for Murphy, but he allows her to go on these errands anytime you ask her to help."

Carwyn wanted to grind his teeth when Tenzin said the word *allow*.

Her eyes lit up. "You really do hate him, don't you?"

"I don't."

"Fine. You hate that he has a tie to her. Hate that she feels a sense of obligation to him."

"Yes." Carwyn tried to find the words that would make sense to Tenzin. "I don't want her to feel an obligation to anyone other than me. And I only want her to feel one toward me because I'd cut off my right arm and give it to her if she wanted it."

Tenzin scrunched up her nose. "I don't think she will ever want to possess your right arm. Or your left one for that matter. Why would she want your arm? I suppose if she wanted a piece of you left if you die—"

"It's a figure of speech, Tenzin." He glanced over his shoulder to see Chloe and Brigid coming back from the women's bathroom. "I'd give her anything she wanted. *Any*thing. Anytime. I don't want her to feel obligated to anyone outside of us."

Tenzin frowned. "But Ben says that's not how it works."

"What?"

Tenzin didn't finish her thought because Brigid and Chloe had returned to the table and Carwyn's phone started buzzing in his pocket. He grabbed the small device wrapped in a heavily insulated case and looked at the number.

"Los Angeles." He looked at Brigid. "Who do we know in Los Angeles?"

Brigid looked at him as if he'd lost his mind. "Besides two of our best friends?"

"Oh right." But Beatrice and Giovanni's number would

34

have come up as listed on his phone. Carwyn was staring at a number that was totally foreign.

Oh, why not? It was probably a telemarketer, but he could have fun with that. He pushed the button and said, "Hello?"

"Father Carwyn?" The voice sounded worried. "Am I speaking to Fath— I'm sorry. Carwyn. I was told you'd left the priesthood."

"Who is this?" He motioned Brigid closer. As long as she was close to the phone, her superior senses would allow her to pick up the man's voice. "Who gave you this number?"

"It was given to me by a priest in Ensenada. A man I trust. I thought he might know... Well, being brushed by the drugs trade, I thought he might have an idea of what I should do. Though there's no evidence that she was involved in anything—"

"I'm sorry," Brigid broke in. "We have no idea who you are. My name is Brigid Connor. I'm Father Carwyn's wife and partner."

"That sounds so weird," Chloe said. "And wrong."

"My name is Father Anthony Clarence at Saint Peter's Holy Church in LA," the man said. "I'm calling to reach Carwyn ap Bryn. I've been told he might be able to help me."

"Help you with what?" Carwyn asked.

"You've reached the correct person," Brigid said. "Take a deep breath. How can we help?"

"Her name is Lupe." The urgency in the man's voice morphed into exhaustion. "Lupe Martínez. And she's already been missing for a week. The police won't do anything. They said she ran away."

Carwyn and Brigid exchanged a look. Unfortunately, running away was an all too common occurrence.

"Can you help me?" Father Anthony said. "The police don't understand. I know this girl. Lupe would never leave her mother like this. She'd never leave her family. I know something is very wrong."

"It's past midnight on the West Coast, Father." Brigid scooted closer to Carwyn. "Why are you calling so late?"

"Am I?" The man's voice dropped to nearly a whisper. "I thought you'd be awake because of the... Well, the... You know. Your particular condition."

Brigid's eyebrows both went up.

Well, well. Carwyn was impressed. Someone trusted Father Anthony not only with Carwyn's number but also with the truth about what kind of creature the priest was.

"Is this a good number to reach you?" Carwyn asked.

"Yes. You can use it anytime. Day or night. I tell my kids that too."

Brigid nodded. "Okay. Give us an hour or two to get back to you. We'll know more then."

Carwyn pushed the End button and looked at his wife. "You feel like taking a road trip?"

"*Don't* get any ideas." Brigid shoved her tiny finger in his face. "This is not me quitting my job. This is me *possibly* helping out a family who needs help because I happen to be on the right continent. I haven't quit my job and I haven't decided anything."

Carwyn nodded. "Duly noted."

"Fine." She reached for her own phone. "Now let's call our contacts in Los Angeles and find out exactly who Father Anthony Clarence of Saint Peter's Church is and why he's so sure this Lupe Martínez needs our help."

CHAPTER FOUR

Los Angeles, California
Three days later

"Like I said, it's been over a week now," Father Anthony Clarence of Saint Peter's Holy Church told Brigid as they walked through the dark streets of downtown Los Angeles. "It's not like her to disappear. Lupe isn't a runaway."

Brigid watched the shadows with eyes that saw far more than the human beside her. "The types of kids who run away might surprise you, Father."

"Hey." He paused and looked Brigid in the eye. "I'm not naive. I've been working among the homeless and addicted in this city far too long to be naive. I know kids run away and I understand the reasons are complicated. I'm still telling you, Lupe isn't the type."

Brigid nodded. She'd seen her fair share of priests over the years, and her gut was telling her Father Anthony was one of the good ones. "I'll take your word for it."

The extent of homelessness in one of the richest countries in the world always astonished Brigid. She'd been in Los Angeles before, but she'd never spent time in the area they were exploring. "How many here are women and children?"

"In this particular park? More than average. It's known as kind of a family place because the mission is nearby. Overall in LA? About thirty percent women. Maybe twenty percent of those are in families. I'm not sure the numbers on children. It's hard to say."

Brigid shook her head. "What's the city doing about it?"

"Not enough. This encampment in the park is pretty quiet. Not a big gang area. Not too many drugs. More families here; people look out for each other, you know? But the city will kick everyone out in a couple of weeks. And a couple of days after they move everyone out, people will be back." Father Anthony gestured toward the mission building glowing in the distance. "We try to fill in the gaps, especially with families. Many aren't on the streets quite yet, but they're living in their cars, drifting from one cheap hotel to another. Staying in unsafe circumstances because they don't want to be on the street."

"Was Lupe ever homeless?" What motivated a girl to work down here two times a week? She could have spent time with her friends. Posted on social media. Taken up a sport. "Was it personal for her?"

Father Anthony opened his mouth, then closed it.

Brigid started walking again, giving the man time to formulate his thoughts.

"It was personal for her." The priest caught up in a few minutes. "Lupe and her mother were never homeless—their extended family is very close—but she knew what it was like not to fit in. She knew what it meant to be out of your element."

"Why?" Brigid spotted a furtive drug deal taking place behind a tent, but she ignored it. There were no weapons, no vulnerables in the area. Who was she to judge how a mortal survived a cold night on the LA streets? "Why did she feel out of place?"

———

"WE DON'T HAVE DOCUMENTS."

Carwyn met Lupe's mother at the church. He worked to put the woman at ease, immediately telling her he was a private investigator, a former priest, and married to a security specialist. María Estrada was eager to speak to anyone who could help find her daughter.

"You didn't come here legally?" Carwyn asked.

The woman spoke near-perfect English and was obviously educated, but Carwyn knew that migration happened for unexpected and unpredictable reasons sometimes. He and Brigid had helped more than one woman escaping domestic violence who hadn't stopped to fill out paperwork.

María Estrada sighed. "When we first came, I thought it would only be for a visit. A few months. Maybe less. Getting a visa can take years, and all I wanted was to see my sister, spend time with her and my brother-in-law after Luis died."

"That's your husband? Lupe's father?"

María nodded. "I was wrecked. A mess. My sister is my best friend. And I didn't have any interest living in the United States, so I thought, I'm not going to go through all the paperwork for a visit. That's ridiculous. But I came here and... a few months turned into a year." María looked to the side. "I helped my sister at her business cleaning houses, so I kept busy and was making money. Lupe... she was like a flower that finally bloomed—she loved her cousins so much. She adored my brother-in-law; Emilio was like a second father to her, and he treated her just like one of his own kids."

Carwyn said, "That must have been comforting after losing her own father, to have an uncle close. It would be hard to take a little girl away from that."

"Yes, exactly. So about a year and a half after we came— Lupe was already in school here and doing so well in her classes—I went back to Mexico, sold our house to the people who'd been renting it, and found a place on the same street as my sister and brother-in-law. Just a room to rent. At that point getting papers seemed impossible, and I think..." María looked away and sighed. "I think in the back of my mind, I thought that when Lupe was older, we'd go back. We had a good life in Mexico before her father passed. Our family there is wonderful. I thought when she was ready for college, we'd move back and go to Mexico City or Guadalajara or one of the big cities. I would have enough savings by then to buy another house—a nicer house in the city—and Lupe could go to university there. The best of both countries, you know? So papers didn't really matter."

"Did Lupe know she was undocumented?"

"Not right away. It's not something we talked about, so until it was time to start thinking about college..."

Carwyn nodded in understanding. "Undocumented students can't apply for financial aid or most scholarships."

María's expression was devastated. "We had the most horrible fight when Lupe realized what that meant for her future. All the schools her peers were talking about? We could never afford them on our own. She changed. She was angry. Stopped speaking to me. She started spending more time on her phone."

"Was she meeting any new people? Making friends you didn't know?"

María crossed her arms. "I don't know. She wouldn't talk to me, and she even cut her aunt and uncle out. She resented her cousins who were legal and making plans for college. She refused to even talk about going to community college—which we could afford—or moving back to Mexico and applying to university there."

"Would you say she started to rebel? Act out in other ways?"

María blinked hard. "Nothing like that. She was just... distant. Quiet. She'd always had a heart for homeless people —always helped out at the church in youth group—but after our fight, she found every excuse to be down there at the mission or at the church. To be away from me, I think. She didn't want anything to do with me."

María lifted her chin and wiped tears from her cheeks. "She's a good girl. The police? They told me that she probably ran off with friends or this boy the father says that she knew from the mission." María shook her head. "She would never. Even if she was angry with me, she wouldn't have disappeared without telling her cousins or her uncle. That's how I know something is very wrong."

"Why didn't you press the police more?" Carwyn asked. "If she doesn't have a pattern of acting out—"

"Why do you think?" María said. "She's just another illegal girl to them. I hear how they talk. They don't know her.

They don't care about her. That's why I asked Father Anthony if he knew any private detectives." The woman looked stricken. "We don't have a lot of money, but you can have all my savings, and if it is more than that, I will work for the rest of my life to pay you and your wife—"

"No." Carwyn put a comforting hand on her arm. "That's not how we work. Not for friends like Father Anthony. We'll find Lupe for you. You don't need to pay us."

María swallowed hard, clearly afraid to be too optimistic. "How?"

Carwyn smiled. "Trust me. My wife is very good at what she does."

————

FATHER ANTHONY WAS PROBABLY CONFUSED by how long and how far Brigid wanted to walk through the streets, but she had her reasons. If this were Dublin, she'd know where to go and who to talk to. But this wasn't Dublin, and she didn't have territorial rights here. They'd cleared their presence through the vampire authorities in the area, but Brigid wasn't about to go around bashing heads and making demands. She wouldn't get any information that way.

The park, the mission, and the surrounding streets, she was learning, were a community. Maybe not a traditional one —and certainly not one without dangers—but there was a structure. As they walked through the streets, Brigid took it all in, absorbing the scents, sounds, and rhythm of the neighborhood into her blood.

There were dealers who had staked out territory. There were sex workers who had regular routes. There were gathering places and voices that rose a little louder than the others. Shouts and quieter voices that calmed the shouting.

Brigid paused and narrowed her attention on a van that had passed them three or four times. "Who is that?"

The van had pulled up at a corner, and the doors were open. A middle-aged woman and a group of teen girls were setting out tables and canvas chairs along with a portable firepit.

"That's Tonya. I don't know much about her background, but she's with Streets Alive, a homeless advocacy program. They pass out blankets and food. Try to connect people with the right services. That sort of thing. They're privately funded like us."

"Did Lupe know her?"

"All the kids know Tonya," Father Anthony said. "She's a regular at the mission, and she knows the kids from Saint Peter's. Looks out for them. The girls especially. They know if they ever get into trouble and I'm not close, they should go to her and she'll call the mission number from there."

"Not the police?"

Father Anthony frowned. "If something criminal happened, we report it. If anyone threatens the kids, we report it. If someone simply gets scared or freaked out or has a run-in with someone really high or mentally ill, they head to Tonya. We try not to call law enforcement unless we absolutely have to."

"Fair enough." Brigid nodded toward Tonya's compound. "I need to speak with her."

They meandered over to Tonya's van where a group of women had gathered around the firepit. The woman named Tonya was a large, middle-aged black woman with silver-threaded curls, wearing a heavy sweatshirt over worn jeans. Beside her was a shrunken older white woman who looked as if she'd lived a very hard life. The older woman was holding a cigarette and one of the girls was staring at it.

As they approached, Tonya narrowed her eyes on Brigid as she and Father Anthony walked closer.

Brigid appreciated the woman's instincts because they were correct. *That's right. I'm a predator, but I'm no threat to you or yours.*

Brigid didn't say it. The woman wouldn't have listened to her words anyway. She knew better, that words meant nothing on the street. Actions were what mattered.

"Tonya?" Father Anthony waited at the edge of the compound for the woman to notice him.

"Padre." Tonya's eyes shifted from scrutinizing Brigid to smiling at Father Anthony. "How you doing tonight?"

"Still worried," he said. "Still no word from Lupe."

"Huh." Tonya reached over for the cigarette the old woman was smoking. She took a drag and handed it back. "That's a shame."

"Actually" —Father Anthony stepped forward, but Brigid waited on the edge of the circle— "Lupe is why we're here tonight. We were hoping—"

"I already talked to the police when they asked me." Tonya examined Brigid, from the black leather boots she wore to her whiskey-brown eyes, which never broke away. Tonya frowned a little, then looked at Father Anthony. "Told them what I knew about the girl."

"I'm not the police." Brigid spoke quietly, but her voice was clear. "And I'm not from around here. But I am looking for Lupe."

Tonya sat back and cocked her head. "Girl, where *are* you from?"

"Dublin," Brigid said. "Ireland."

"That's some accent."

The corner of Brigid's mouth turned up. "I could say the same thing about you."

Tonya threw her head back and laughed. "I think I like you. I only understand about every third word you say, mind, but I like you." Tonya's eyes were shrewd. "So what interest does *your kind* have with that girl?"

Brigid felt one eyebrow rise. "My kind?"

Tonya leaned back and seemed to pick something from behind her upper canine tooth.

Brigid got the message loud and clear. Tonya knew about vampires. Interesting, but not that surprising if she worked on the street.

"Yeah," Tonya said. "Your kind."

Brigid smiled a little and glanced at the small group around the fire. "You mean... the Irish?"

Tonya reached for her neighbor's cigarette and took another drag, her hooded eyes never leaving Brigid. "Yeah. The... Irish." She glanced at one of the teenage girls with her. "Miss Lettie, would you mind giving our Irish guest your seat for a moment so we can talk?"

The girl stood up, and Brigid noticed she was pregnant.

"Yes, ma'am. I have some studying I can do in the van."

"Good girl." Tonya kicked the empty chair next to her. "Sit, my *Irish* friend. Let's talk."

Brigid glanced around the fire. The older woman was staring into the flames and nursing her cigarette. One of the teenagers was glued to her phone, and the other one appeared nearly asleep.

She took the offered seat and angled her shoulders toward Tonya. "I'm sure you're wondering why I'm interested in Lupe."

"Yep. And don't try to bullshit me."

Not when I need your cooperation so dearly. "I'm a private security specialist from Dublin."

"Private security specialist." Tonya reached for a pack of cigarettes and lit a fresh one. "Sounds expensive."

"I am. Normally I work for a very rich man who pays me lots of money to oversee the security for his business, but right now I'm here as a favor."

Tonya nodded. "Fair enough. Who's the favor for?"

"Me," Father Anthony said. "I called a friend who called a friend."

"My husband was a priest in a former life."

"Is your husband also... Irish?"

The corner of Brigid's mouth turned up. "In your meaning of the word? Yes. But don't tell him I called him that."

"And he was a priest, huh?" Tonya pursed her lips. "Never heard that one before."

"Carwyn is speaking with Lupe's mother right now."

Tonya shook her head. "Poor woman. She's a good girl, Lupe."

"So you don't think she ran away?"

Tonya paused. "Well, there's running away, then there's running away."

Brigid reached for the box of cigarettes, and Tonya handed it over. "Tell me more."

CHAPTER FIVE

"Lupe's got a big heart," Tonya said. "That can be good and bad if you know what I mean."

"I do." Brigid had seen more than one good-hearted person break themselves on the rocks of another person's pain. "Big heart to work with people here?"

"Big heart for *everyone*. She was always a generous girl, but in the past year, she seemed... on edge. Like she finally realized how fucked up the world really is, you know? Homelessness. The environment. Immigrant rights. She'd spend all this time reading on her phone and I'd find her crying in one of my chairs."

"She let herself get overwhelmed."

Tonya nodded and blew out a thin stream of smoke. "I can tell you know how it is. You gotta focus on what you can do, not on everything that needs to be done." Tonya tapped her temple with a finger. "That's a recipe for a breakdown. You gonna work in the hard places in this city? You gotta focus on the week you're in. The people you're with right then."

"I understand." Brigid had spent too much time focusing on her own survival to sacrifice herself for those who didn't want to be helped. "You take care of these girls."

Tonya nodded toward the van where the pregnant teen had retreated. "Am I gonna solve teenage pregnancy in LA? Fuck no. But I can make sure Lettie finishes school and doesn't go back into the system with a baby. I can make sure if she wants to keep that baby, she finds what she needs to build a life and not find herself in a dead end."

"I get what you're saying, but what does that have to do with—"

"Lupe met Daniel when he was working with me, so I guess I feel a little responsible. And Daniel..." She took a drag on her cigarette. "Daniel's a lot like Lupe. He cares. But he's also angry."

Okay, now we're getting somewhere. "Anger can be useful. Tell me more about Daniel."

"He was another one with a good heart. That's why I kept him around even when he pissed me off."

"Was this Daniel messing around with Lupe?"

"Nah, he knew better." Tonya shook her head. "I think she probably had a little crush on him, but he knows not to shit where he eats. That boy is twenty, and he knows I'd have his balls if I found out he was fooling with any of these girls."

The teen who'd been messing around on her phone spoke, not once looking up. "All Daniel cares about is like... fucking the system. He doesn't have girlfriends."

Brigid asked, "But Lupe is sweet for him?"

The girl frowned. "What?"

"Does she *like* him? Romantically?"

The girl rolled her eyes. "I guess. I mean, she kind of

knows how Daniel is, but she kind of doesn't, you know? Lupe's like, really naive. Super nice and not full of herself, not like some of the girls from Saint Pete's, but like, still really innocent and stuff."

The other girl, who'd looked like she was sleeping, said, "Lupe's mom doesn't let her date or anything. I don't think she's even kissed a guy."

Tonya snorted. "And what's that worth? You think it's any kind of thing to let a man put his mouth on you? Girl, go in the van with Lettie and do your homework—I knew you was faking."

The sleepy girl opened her eyes, and the corner of her mouth turned up. "They left together. Lupe and Daniel. That night she disappeared? She went with him; everyone knows it."

The other girl cackled. "She probably got more than a kiss by now."

Both the teenagers were snickering, but Brigid was taking furious mental notes. "Daniel was with your organization," she said to Tonya. "I'm going to need a last name. I don't want to drag you into this, but it'd be faster to track him down if you can get us his name, where he lived, any kind of—"

"They were planning something." Tonya leaned forward. "Some protest or *action* or something. I heard them whispering about it. Children thinking they so sneaky." Tonya huffed. "I don't know what it was, but I don't think they ran away together. Not like that. And I don't want either of them to get in trouble. She's naive, but she knows her own mind. And Daniel wouldn't have forced her to do anything she didn't want to do."

"Fair enough," Brigid said. "I'm not interested in getting

them into trouble. I'm more worried about whatever they were planning and if they got in over their heads."

Tonya nodded slowly. "You got a piece of paper?"

Brigid withdrew the notebook that lived in her leather jacket. "As a matter of fact, I do."

———

"DANIEL SIVA," Brigid read from her notebook as they drove to their friends' house in Pasadena. "He has a record, but only for minor drug possession and one disorderly conduct in some place called Indio. I don't know where that is." She glanced at him. "So odd to see you driving a car."

"It's been a while." Carwyn leaned back and navigated the Los Angeles streets in his friend Giovanni's classic Mustang. Classic cars lacked the digital technology prevalent in newer cars and were far easier for vampires to drive. "It's a bit cramped though. Must be built for an Italian."

"Ha ha."

"Indio is out near Palm Springs. Is that where this Daniel is from?"

"Tonya says he has a sister here in LA, but she thought his mom lived somewhere out in the desert. So maybe?"

"And no idea where his house is?"

"No." Brigid continued reading through the notes she'd taken when she was out with Father Anthony. "Tonya said Daniel was involved in all sorts of causes. Homelessness, immigration, animal rights, the environment."

"Immigrant rights could have been something Lupe was drawn to considering her legal status."

"I wouldn't be surprised. I wonder if Daniel knew Lupe's

situation. Tonya said he worked for at least four organizations she knew of."

"Busy lad keeping himself occupied."

Brigid tapped on her notepad. "Drug possession on his record. He might be in recovery."

Carwyn had known more than one addict in recovery—including his darling wife—who couldn't abide being idle. Idle time meant space to think about getting high.

"None of the organizations he worked for will be open at this hour," Carwyn said. "Do you want me to try to stay awake in the morning and give them a call?" He'd be groggy, but he could manage, unlike Brigid. At her age, she was out with the sunrise.

"Don't be silly," Brigid said. "I'll ask Beatrice."

"Oh right. Good idea."

The friends they were staying with were not only vampires but also some of Carwyn's oldest friends. They were also investigators in their own way, though their business had more to do with retrieving rare books and the odd document that immortals misplaced over the centuries.

Giovanni and Beatrice had impeccable connections in Los Angeles. Beatrice was also a day-walker, an immortal genetic quirk related to her vampire sire. Uncommon, but not unheard of.

"Beatrice usually has half a day to kill at least," Brigid said. "Might as well give her something to do. And her great-great-great-grandfather is the vampire in charge of the city. She'll know the right people to call."

"In addition to information about this young man" — Carwyn angled his shoulders to try to get more comfortable — "can Beatrice see about a more comfortable vehicle?"

"Something along the lines of a monster truck?"

Carwyn's eyes lit up. "You brilliant woman. Can we?"

Brigid laughed. "You're mad; we'd never find parking."

"We're not going to be driving during rush hour. We're dead to the world all day."

Brigid sighed. "Don't remind me. I have a feeling that's going to complicate this case. Too many humans involved."

Personally, Carwyn considered vampire sleep one of the highest benefits of immortality. There was no chance of insomnia or restless sleep. You were awake or you were out. It suited his personality beautifully.

He eyed his wife with some satisfaction. "Enjoying yourself?"

She gave him a sideways glance. "Enjoying myself seems like an odd way to put it when we're trying to track down a missing girl."

"Have you talked to Murphy and Tom tonight?"

She looked out the window. "Called them when we woke up."

"And?"

Brigid crossed her arms. "And nothing exciting is happening in Dublin—is that what you want to hear? The most excitement they've had is a visit from a manufacturer in Ghana who'd like to produce a new kind of shell for Murphy's hardware. Are you happy?"

"Are you?" Carwyn kept strict control of the smile that wanted to erupt. "All I'm trying to point out is that you're out here, doing good in the world, while business back in Dublin is proceeding exactly as it should with a security team that's more than competent."

"Are you saying they don't need me?"

Trick question, Carwyn! Do not walk into the trap.

"I'm saying…" He smiled slowly. "That the organization and updates you've set in place have allowed Dublin to operate as one of the safest cities in the vampire world."

There. Avoided that hazard handily. Nicely done, self.

The corner of Brigid's mouth twitched. "What a diplomat you are."

"I only speak the truth. Who knows? Maybe Lupe would enjoy studying in Dublin. She seems a very bright girl."

"Hmmm." Brigid turned her eyes back to the road. "What is that girl up to? What was she thinking?"

"You've been a teenage girl far more recently than I have, so you're going to have to take the lead on that question."

"Ha!" Brigid shook her head. "I was a mad, angry little thing. I didn't think about anyone but myself. Lupe sounds like the kind of girl who hoists the whole world on her shoulders and is determined to carry it."

"Maybe that's where we start then." Carwyn steered the car off the highway and onto the quiet, dark streets of Pasadena. "Who did Lupe think needed her help?"

"Oh dear." Brigid sighed. "That could be a problem."

"Is it?"

Brigid opened her phone again and looked for something.

Carwyn brought the car to a stop at a light and she held out the screen for him to see. "Who's that?"

"That's Daniel Siva, the boy she disappeared with."

Carwyn groaned. "Dark, brooding boy with long locks and soulful eyes. Drug possession. Are we guessing he has a tortured past?"

"I don't know if he does or not," Brigid said. "But if Lupe thought Daniel needed her help, do you think she'd refuse?"

"I've read too many romance novels to doubt you." He steered the car toward the exclusive enclave of San Marino and the walled estates where his friends had found safety and anonymity in the middle of the city. "I think your instincts are right. If we find Daniel Siva, we're going to find Lupe Martínez."

———

IT WAS close to dawn when Brigid exited the spa-like bathroom in the guesthouse at Giovanni and Beatrice's place. She walked out of the bedroom and into the living area, looking for her husband while she rubbed a towel over her short crop of hair.

"Carwyn?"

"Outside!"

She stayed barefoot and walked out to the garden, but she still couldn't spot her mate. "Where are you?"

She didn't hear Carwyn, but he sent a tickle of energy through the blood bond they shared. She turned to the left and headed behind the guesthouse and down a short hill covered in various species of palm trees.

The rustle of the breeze soughing through the leaves brushed her ears like silk against skin. The night was deep and silent around her, and the only sound was the wind through the palms. The thin nightshirt she wore fluttered against her hips, and the night air was cool on her bare legs.

She sensed him before she heard him. She turned to the right and smiled a second before he tackled her to the ground, caging her body with his so she felt nothing of the impact but the soft ground against her back and his mouth capturing hers.

The earth curved around them, moving as her mate commanded it. He wore a pair of loose pants and nothing else. His chest was sprinkled with red hair, and his body bore the scars of human life and immortality married to a fire vampire.

She was past worrying about the scars she sometimes left when her element overtook her. Carwyn didn't seem to mind the sting, and more often than not, he provoked it.

In the dark shadows of the palms, he tugged her shirt up and over her head, latching his mouth to the sensitive rise of her breasts.

Brigid closed her eyes and wiggled out of her clothes as her mate feasted on her. His fangs nicked the sensitive underside of one breast, making her gasp. She scented the blood rising to the surface and the slow, leisurely pull of his mouth and tongue as he fed from her.

The earth beneath her back hummed with energy, pushing her into his arms. Carwyn sealed the delicate wound and worked his mouth down her body, tasting the hidden corners and angles she covered with armor through the night.

She had no armor with him. None. He stripped her bare, and she came back every night for more. He was her own personal supplicant, worshipping her body as he knit her soul together a little more with every passing night.

"Beloved." He breathed against her skin and his mouth dipped between her legs and Brigid's back bowed in pleasure. "Beloved."

Brigid adored him with a love that bordered on idolatry. As he brought her to climax, she saw stars behind her eyes and felt her skin heat against the damp morning air. Steam rose as Carwyn rose over her, kissing her mouth as she pushed him to his back and straddled his hips.

Her fangs were sharp and aching in her mouth. She lost all sense of control, shoving his pants down his hips and driving her body onto his as he bowed up from the earth and caught her by the nape, pressing her mouth to his neck.

"Bite." He commanded her in a low voice, and she obeyed.

Brigid's teeth pierced the heated skin of his neck, and his rich, ancient blood entered her as she rode his body toward climax.

CHAPTER SIX

Famed vampire Giovanni Vecchio was juggling a headstrong six-year-old, a formidable nanny, and a barking puppy when Carwyn found his old friend the following night in the main living room.

"Carwyn!" Giovanni spotted him and his eyes lit up. "Excellent. Can you help me with…" He motioned generally to the chaos around him.

Carwyn picked his niece up by her ankles and lifted her as she burst into giggles. "Giovanni, what possessed you to get this strange chew toy for the new dog? It doesn't look like it would taste very good, even for a Labrador. And we all know they're not picky about food."

Sadia Vecchio, Giovanni and Beatrice's daughter, had been adopted before she was two. She didn't remember when vampires weren't a part of her life, and Carwyn and Brigid were a fixture. "Uncle Carwyn, I'm not a chew toy!"

Dema, Sadia's nanny, watched from the doorway as Percy, the half-grown black lab that had joined the family four months ago, ran in circles and yapped.

Carwyn glanced at Dema. "How's the training going?"

"Dog training?" Dema shook her head. "That's Zain's department, not mine. I wrangle the child; he wrangles the dog."

"Speaking of Zain, I was wondering if I might speak to him about borrowing a vehicle while we're here."

Giovanni frowned. "The Mustang isn't a good fit?"

Dema started laughing. "Shoulders, Gio. Look at him."

The Italian shrugged. Though he was tall and broadly built for a five-hundred-year-old European, his blood was from warmer climes. He looked miniature compared to Carwyn's bulk.

"Talk to Zain," Giovanni said. "He'll be able to connect you with something. A pickup truck maybe?"

"I am voting for a monster truck," Carwyn said, swinging Sadia back and forth. "Brigid seems to think it's a bad idea for some reason."

Giovanni pointed to the girl. "If she vomits, you're cleaning it up."

Carwyn flipped the girl upright. Her eyes were going in two directions. "There you go, Sadia, my girl. I suppose you're not a chew toy after all."

Giovanni said, "Sadia, can you take Perseus in the back-yard so Baba and Uncle Carwyn can talk please?"

"Okay." She ran toward the french doors, bumping into only one side table on the way toward the backyard. "Percy, come!"

Dema followed them and closed the doors behind her.

Giovanni closed his eyes. "The quiet."

"Whose idea was it to get a dog?"

"Sadia's. And Zain backed her up, the betrayer."

Giovanni and Beatrice's driver, chef, and man-about-town was Zain. When both parents were vampires, day staff was a necessity. Zain was an excellent human and a bang-up chef. Carwyn would have hired him in a minute.

"Good pup. You can't go wrong with a well-trained Labrador."

"Where are your hounds these days?"

Carwyn had bred and raised Irish wolfhounds for centuries. "Wicklow. I handed the mob over to Deirdre's foreman at the farm since Brigid and I are traveling so much. I miss them, but they're happy as pigs in mud."

Giovanni raised a curious eyebrow. "Any progress on what we were talking about last month?"

"I brought up the idea of quitting in New York." He sank into a chair opposite the fire. "She's considering it."

"Things like what you're doing here are far more her strength," Giovanni said. "There's no challenge left for her in Dublin. The city runs like a well-oiled machine."

"I know."

"Hmm." Giovanni crossed his arms. "Perhaps Beatrice can convince her."

"One thing's for certain," Carwyn said. "She'll make up her own mind about it and that's that. She's not looking for advice from me or anyone."

"NO, I'D *LOVE* YOUR ADVICE," Brigid said. She and Beatrice were in the library to do some work on the computer loaded with the voice-activated Nocht system that Brigid's boss had designed for vampire use.

"I don't know how much help I can be," Beatrice said. "I've never been in your situation. When I quit working at the library here, it was a necessity. I couldn't work at a human research library as a vampire. And I didn't have the same loyalty to my employers there."

"Exactly. I know Carwyn and Murphy don't get along. I know they've always annoyed each other. I just don't know why that's supposed to be my problem."

"It's not," Beatrice said. "It's theirs. They're grown men, for goodness' sake. Don't let them convince you that it should be your issue." She got out her heavy, plastic-encased computer and set it on the library table.

"It's just that..." Brigid thought hard. "I can't forget that I was a mess. I was an addict, and he gave me a chance. Working for Murphy was my lifeline for years. It kept me sane. Working with Tom and Declan... I mean, I've never had brothers, but it feels a bit like I do when I'm working with them. I feel like I'm part of something important."

"And you're worried that if you quit working for Murphy, you won't have that anymore?"

"I won't. I'm not saying they won't be friends, or even that they'd resent my decision—I don't think they would—but it wouldn't be the same."

Beatrice opened her computer and stared at the screen. "I can see that."

"I'd be on my own. I'd have Carwyn of course, but I wouldn't have a team." Brigid blinked. "Fuck me!"

Beatrice frowned. "What?"

"I just realized something."

"What? That you're secretly in love with me and we should leave our annoying husbands and run away together to form a female-only immortal island like Wonder Woman but with vampires?"

"No— Well...?" Brigid nodded. "Tempting, but no. I just realized I'm a team player. I like having a team."

"Oh. Yes. I agree, you work well in collaboration."

"Anything you need to talk about? That island fantasy seemed pretty well planned out."

"No... Maybe? No." Beatrice opened a notebook and started scrolling through something on the computer, her hands in specialized gloves. "I'm okay. Six-year-olds and puppies are exhausting, especially in combination."

"That tracks." Brigid nodded at the computer. "Any news?"

"I heard back from my grandfather's security guy. Daniel Siva doesn't show up on any of their radars, so whatever he's involved in, it's likely unrelated to anything immortal. That's good and bad. Probably less dangerous for the missing girl, but also less information I can offer you on tracking him down. Do you need to get into LAPD's system?"

"Oh no, Declan already got me inside there. It's not very secure."

Beatrice laughed. "Yeah. I know. So what are you guys going to do about finding this guy?"

"Old-fashioned legwork, it appears," Brigid said. "We'll be needing a car. Hopefully one that fits my husband's shoulders if that's possible."

Beatrice pursed her lips. "Have you thought about renting a monster truck?"

"Not you too."

———

ZAIN HELD the keys out with a grim look on his face. "Bring it back with a scratch and you're repainting it yourself. I just had it detailed."

Carwyn felt his heart sing. It wasn't a monster truck, but it was close. "Is that a matte black 1970 Ford Bronco?"

"Yes, it is." Zain got in Carwyn's space. He wasn't as large as the Welshman, but he was tall and thick in the chest. His neat locks were tied back in the low knot he wore when he was cooking or lifting weights. "It's my father's 1970 Bronco, to be exact. It's also been completely rebuilt so it runs like a dream and the suspension isn't shit. The interior is all new. The seats are custom. This is my baby, Carwyn."

Carwyn tore his eyes away. "I will care for it as if it were my own, my muscle-bound friend. How much do you want for it?"

"It's *not* for sale." Zain slapped the keys against Carwyn's chest. "Do I need to give Brigid the speech too?"

"Oh no, she doesn't drive in this country except on a motorbike. The steering wheel on the wrong side is more than she wants to deal with."

He heard Brigid approach from behind.

"Oh, that's beautiful!" she exclaimed. "Can I drive it?"

"No," Zain said. "It's mine and you're Irish."

"Feck off." She scowled. "What's that got to do with— Oh, the steering wheel thing, right?"

Carwyn and Zain both nodded.

Brigid shrugged. "Aye, that's fair. I always hate when Yanks drive in Dublin. Feckin' awful, all of you."

Carwyn turned to Zain. "I promise I will take care of it for you. Much appreciated."

"Fine." He glanced at Carwyn. Then Brigid. Back to Carwyn. "Don't let her drive."

"I won't ask!" Brigid scowled. "See if I let you shoot any of my guns when you visit Dublin next time."

"That's just mean, Brigid." Zain smiled and walked back to the kitchen. "Don't wreck my car!"

"So what's on the agenda for the night?" Carwyn asked.

"We're hitting the streets in your monster truck and asking questions. I have names." She waved a piece of paper. "Beatrice did manage to get at least one name and address from every place Daniel worked. First order of business? We need to know where he was living."

"You realize he might have been homeless too. Or living in a van. Something like that."

"Don't think so," Brigid said. "One of the people Beatrice talked to mentioned a garage apartment, so I think he had a place, and it's possible Lupe is there."

They walked to the Bronco, and Carwyn helped Brigid into the passenger seat.

"Carwyn," Brigid said, "would you call me a team player or a—?"

"Team player," Carwyn said. "Definitely." He walked around and jumped into the Bronco on the other side. "Why are you frowning?"

"It's just annoying when you know things about me that I don't realize about myself."

"I can't help it that I'm an emotional genius, Brigid." He tried to keep a straight face. "This is why you should always listen to me. About everything."

She snorted. "Feck off."

"It's okay." He started the car. "Don't try to compare yourself. That's not fair to *you*."

"God save me from egotistical Welshmen."

"It'll be all right." He reached over and squeezed her hand. "Let it out."

————

"DANNY?" The freshly pressed director of CleanUPLA was incredulous. "You think Danny ran away with a teenage girl?"

"We're not the police," Brigid said quickly. "And he's not in any trouble. We don't think he kidnapped her or anything like that. We just need to find the girl. Her mother is sick with worry, as you can imagine."

The woman named Sarah held the picture of Lupe. "I don't recognize her; Danny never brought her around. Honestly, I never saw him with anyone in a romantic way, you know? There was a girl in the office who was into him and asked him out—supercute girl, you know? He wasn't interested. I thought maybe he was ace or something." She backtracked. "Not because of the girl. He just struck me as... uninterested. I guess that's the word. He never talked about past relationships or anything. He was totally focused on the work."

"Do you have any idea where he lived?"

"I mean, he was a volunteer for us, so we don't have any paperwork really." She closed her eyes. "I'm pretty sure he lived in South Park because we picked him up at the rec center there a few times, and he always looked like... Fresh, you know? Like he'd just cleaned up."

"Thank you," Brigid said. "Did he have any particular friends at CleanUPLA that you can think of?"

She narrowed her eyes. "Maybe Phil. He's an older guy. Old hippy, you know? I have his number if you want it."

"That would be helpful," Carwyn said. "Thank you."

They wrote down Phil's number and tried calling, but no one picked up. Brigid left a message and her number before she hung up.

"Next?"

They drove to a tidy residential street in Willowbrook, far from the mansions in San Marino but miles away from the hard streets of downtown. It was a quiet family neighborhood and home to the director of the Downtown Revival Coalition, a man called Roderick Jordan.

Carwyn and Brigid parked on a street lined by practical compact cars and a few small trucks. They walked toward the front door of the Jordan house and heard a deep bark greeting them.

Brigid pressed the doorbell and hung back from the front step as footsteps approached the door. A tall black man holding a toddler opened the front door but left the screen closed. A large grey dog sat dutifully at his feet.

"Can I help you?"

Carwyn said, "Good Lord, you have the lowest voice I've ever heard. Even lower than the man in the insurance commercials."

Brigid looked at her husband, shaking her head. "Seriously?"

"What? It's true!" Carwyn pointed to the man, who looked amused. "I bet he's heard that before."

The man laughed a little. "Yeah, I have. I don't want to be

rude or anything, but my wife's nearly got dinner on the table. Are you selling something or...?"

"Excuse my knob of a husband," Brigid said. "Are you Roderick Jordan from the Downtown Revival Coalition?"

The man nodded. "Can I help you?"

"We're looking for information about Daniel Siva, and we were given your name as a contact. I hope you don't mind that we found you at home."

The man shrugged. "Nah, it's cool. Is Daniel in trouble or something?"

"We hope not," Carwyn said. "We're private investigators hired by a mother over in Huntington Park. Her daughter worked with Daniel sometimes over at Saint Peter's rescue mission. Do you know it?"

Roderick nodded. "Yeah, I know the mission. Have you talked to Tonya Parker?"

"I have," Brigid said. "We know Daniel volunteered with your organization quite a few times. Is that how he became connected? Through Tonya?"

"Yeah, I know Tonya from way back. She and my mom are friends. I wasn't too sure about Daniel at first, but Tonya vouched for him."

Brigid asked, "Why? Was something off about Daniel when you met him?"

Roderick shifted the little boy from one hip to the other. The dog remained at attention. "Uh, you know, he was just real quiet. I don't want to say secretive, 'cause that sounds negative and he might just be real private. Passed the standard background check. Had a little drug use in his past, but he said he'd been in recovery for about three years, which... Hey, you gotta give people second chances, right?"

"Absolutely," Brigid said.

"Daniel was a hard worker, I can tell you that. He did a lot of park cleanup projects and graffiti cleanups with us. We spent a whole day down at the river one time. It was summer and just scorching. The man didn't slow down once." Roderick narrowed his eyes. "I think he was from the desert, you know? Like Hesperia or Mojave or something like that. I remember him saying he grew up in the heat. Why are you looking for him?"

"Unfortunately, we think our client's daughter might have run off with Daniel. Her name is Guadalupe Martínez. As you can imagine, her mother is worried sick." Brigid stepped closer and showed the picture of Lupe to Roderick. "I don't suppose she looks familiar? She would have been with Daniel a little over a week ago?"

Roderick looked between Carwyn and Brigid a few times. "You know what? Come on in for a minute. Let me ask my wife, Tisha. People talk to her about everything." He nudged the dog back and opened the screen door. "Duke, bed."

The dog promptly retreated back into the house.

"Yeah, there's something about that picture that seems familiar." Roderick motioned them inside. "If anyone knows, it'll be Tisha."

CHAPTER SEVEN

Carwyn was bouncing a laughing baby on his knee and happily tearing into a plate of meat loaf as Brigid and Tisha Jordan spoke.

"Oh my God, I do recognize her." Tisha scooped a serving of green beans onto Carwyn's plate. "She was in Daniel's truck and I remember asking him who she was because he never talked about girls, you know?"

"We've heard he was very private," Brigid said.

"He was *so* private. I could barely get him to talk and everyone talks to me."

Roderick nodded. "Hundred percent true. My girl can make anyone spill."

Tisha smiled at her husband. "It's a gift. I was teasing him a little for bringing a girl around, and then I noticed that she looked about fifteen, so then I was being *real* nosy if you know what I mean."

"I do," Brigid said. "She's seventeen, but what did Daniel say?"

"Just that it wasn't like that. She was a friend's sister, and he was giving her a lift. The girl didn't look worried or anything. She was texting on her phone, so I didn't think much of it."

"Had you seen him with anyone in his truck before? Did he carry people around much?"

"Oh..." She shrugged. "Every now and then. Usually men though. He'd take people he knew from the mission if they needed to get somewhere, like to a probation meeting or a doctor's appointment, stuff like that. Daniel could be a little abrasive, but he had a big heart."

Roderick nodded. "He was very passionate about making the world a better place. That was clear from the beginning. He used to talk about fighting the system. Not letting the system beat him." Roderick took a bite of his dinner. "He was young. Had a feeling he'd had a hard time of things growing up."

"That's the impression we've gotten from a few people," Carwyn said. "Tisha, I don't suppose you know where Daniel lives?"

"I don't know exactly, but I got him talking one time because I was real worried he was on the street and I didn't want that. Especially for someone in recovery, that's very risky. And he told me he had a garage he rented from a friend. It sounded pretty basic, but that made me feel better."

"Did he tell you the friend's name?"

"Oh, it was something real average. Bill? Phil!" Tisha raised a finger. "That's what it was. Pretty sure anyway. Phil. Or Bill, but I'm pretty sure it was Phil. He knew him from another charity he volunteered with."

"That name matches what someone else said. Thank you so much." Brigid started to get up, but Tisha stopped her.

"You've gotta stay for dinner now." She smiled at Carwyn. "Besides, you take that one away and I'll be juggling Dashel instead of enjoying my meal."

Brigid smiled. "Then we'll definitely stay. Feel free to put him to work too. He's excellent at lifting heavy things."

"You're so kind, wife."

"Just trying to keep you out of trouble."

Roderick smiled at Carwyn. "So where are y'all from? Irish or something, right?"

Brigid laughed. "I'm Irish. He's 'or something.'"

Carwyn shook his head and spoke to the baby. "I see we're going to have to educate your father about the long and storied history of my homeland, young man."

———

AFTER BIDDING the Jordan family a good night and exchanging numbers—they promised to call if they heard from Daniel—Carwyn and Brigid were once again on the road.

"We need to find Phil." Brigid's foot was tapping rapidly. "Lupe disappeared on Thursday night. Tisha is pretty sure the last time she saw Daniel—with Lupe in the car—was Friday afternoon because she mentioned getting a babysitter for a date night. Maybe it was a Saturday, but likely Friday…"

"And Daniel lives somewhere in South Park, and his landlord is a man named Phil. We think." Carwyn steered the Bronco into traffic. "Try calling Beatrice. There can't be that many old hippies named Phil in South Park."

"Good idea."

Two phone calls later, Brigid had an address that matched

with a name and number in South Park, along with Phil Macedo's short rap sheet and longer credit history.

"Looks like Phil had a colorful youth." Brigid read from her phone. "Growing pot. Dealing pot. Using pot."

"I'm sensing a theme."

"Nothing recent though." Brigid scrolled down. "He owns his house in South Park and another couple of rental properties in the area. A small apartment complex in Ladera Heights." Brigid looked up. "Seems he's quite wealthy."

"Interesting." Carwyn glanced over. "So Old Hippie Phil is part of the landlord class, eh? Wonder if Daniel-who-hates-the-system knows about that."

"He's Phil's tenant, so I have to imagine he does."

"But there's a difference between renting a garage to your mate and renting out apartments and houses all over Los Angeles if you know what I mean."

"I suppose." Brigid wrinkled her nose. "Is this you showing your age? Pent-up aggression against the land-owning gentry and all that?"

Carwyn raised an eyebrow. "Do you think I owned land when I was human?"

"I suppose I never really thought about it."

"I didn't." He shook his head. "The land owned me. The church was the only sense of freedom I had. My faith and my family were mine; that was all. Didn't even own my horse. That belonged to the local lord along with everything else."

They'd never really talked about it. Brigid had been born into the middle class and had bought her own small house in Dublin before she and Carwyn married. Now they owned a rolling estate on the edge of the city and another cottage in Wicklow near Carwyn's daughter Deirdre's family home.

"Carwyn?"

"Hmm?"

"What was the first home you bought?"

He frowned. "You mean for myself?"

"Yes."

"Not for one of the children or the clan?"

"Just for yourself. Your first home."

He frowned. "I suppose the one I bought for us when we married."

"Our home now?" She was flabbergasted. "You've been alive over a thousand years and you bought your first home eight years ago?"

"Well, I always had homes. Deirdre and Ioan's farm, Isabel and Gustavo's ranch in Cochamó, Gemma's various houses over the years."

"But you never bought—?"

"What would be the point of buying a house to live in by myself?" He looked at her as if she were daft. "It's not a home unless there's people you love living in it."

Fuck, he was so damn sweet even when he didn't mean to be. What was she supposed to do with him? Luckily, they pulled up to Phil's modest one story before Brigid could start getting emotional.

"There're lights on."

Brigid cracked the Bronco door open. "Ah, and a distinctive aroma in the air."

Carwyn grinned. "Some things don't need to change, now do they?"

Brigid walked up the front step and rapped at the door. A few minutes later and a few muffled coughs told her Phil was looking through the door.

Brigid put on her friendliest I'm-not-a-scary-vampire face. "Mr. Macedo? We're friends of Daniel's. We were hoping to speak to you."

There was a long silence, and Brigid could hear him backing away from the door.

She switched to Irish and turned to Carwyn. "He's going to try to run."

"Isn't he near seventy?"

"I think so, but he does not want to speak to us."

Carwyn sighed. "I'll go around back."

The giant man slid into the shadows and remarkably seemed to disappear. He could be an awfully sneaky bastard when he wanted to be. Brigid rapped on the door another time, peeking through the windows to peer inside.

"Mr. Macedo?" She knocked again. "My name's Brigid Connor. I was hoping..." She trailed off when she heard grunting and cursing from the backyard.

She stepped to the left and entered through a wrought iron gate that led to an overgrown backyard that Brigid was guessing far exceeded the personal growing guidelines for marijuana in California.

She saw Phil pinned to the ground by her husband. "Oh Phil. I promise we do not care about your weed."

"Then why are you lying?" The man panted.

"How do you know we're lying?"

"You said— Ow!" Phil tried to shift Carwyn's weight off him. "You said you were friends of Daniel's. And that's bull-shit. Daniel doesn't have any friends."

Brigid crouched down. "That may be, but he does have an apartment here, doesn't he?"

Phil looked to the right. "Maybe."

73

"We're going to look in Daniel's apartment now, Phil." Brigid pulled out Lupe's picture. "And you're going to tell us everything you know about Daniel, Lupe, and what they were doing."

———

"I DON'T KNOW MUCH," Phil said. "There was something going on out in the desert. Some 'action' that Daniel kept talking about. The girl wanted in. They went out there over a week ago. That's all I know."

"An action? What does that mean?" Carwyn asked. "Like a protest?"

"No." Phil shook his head as he led them to Daniel's garage. "Daniel wasn't into protesting. An action would be something like... I don't know. Like if you were really into animal rights, setting all the animals in a lab free. Stuff like that."

"Was Daniel passionate about animal rights?"

"Not that I know of." Phil took out a ring of keys and unlocked the door. "It would have been something with homelessness maybe. Putting up a barricade to save an encampment? Physically protecting an environmental site? Something like that. Daniel spent over three months at the action in Standing Rock."

Brigid turned to Carwyn. "Standing Rock?"

"The Lakota people," Carwyn said. "The ones protecting their water rights from the oil pipeline?"

"Right." Brigid poked her head in the door. "So Daniel was there, was he?"

Phil sounded bored. "Yeah, he talked about it all the time.

Said he put his body on the line for that. He's part Native, I think. Not Lakota though."

"All the same struggle," Carwyn said. "Protecting ancestral lands is every person's responsibility."

Brigid raised an eyebrow. "Look at Himself—eight years in Ireland has made a nationalist of you. Or whatever the Welsh version of that is."

Carwyn rolled his eyes. "Can we focus on the task at hand please?"

"So serious." Brigid felt elated. They were finally making progress. She flipped on the overhead light and saw the living space of a highly organized individual. The bed was made and an air mattress and sleeping bag were rolled at the base of the bed.

Brigid nudged it with her foot. "I'm betting he slept on the air mattress. Gave Lupe the bed."

"They definitely didn't share." Carwyn filled the small garage. "He reads a lot."

Makeshift bookcases and been set up on what looked like old storage shelves. Economics textbooks. Philosophy classics like Aristotle's *Ethics* and Plato's *The Republic*. Karl Marx sat next to Adam Smith, which was next to Orson Scott Card and Tolkien.

"He was curious." Brigid looked through the books, marking which ones looked more worn than others. Many of them came from the Junipero Serra Branch Library on South Main. "Used his library card on the regular."

"He'd read anything. I think all the kid did was read," Phil said. "He worked, he volunteered, and he read books. No friends over. No women. No men. There was one lady who came by once, but I don't remember who she was. They fought and she never came by again."

"His sister, maybe?" Carwyn's voice was soft.

"Maybe."

"Where did he work?" Carwyn asked.

"For a cleaning company," Phil said. "Mostly nights. Some weekends. He volunteered a lot during the afternoons. Slept in the mornings."

Brigid had noticed the lack of windows, thinking it would be a dreary place to live, but if the man had to sleep during the day, the darkness was likely welcome.

She saw a few telltale signs that pointed toward a young man in recovery. The strict cleanliness. The spartan accommodations. The sense of routine. Other than the bed and dresser, the books, and a small refrigerator, the only thing of note was the modest exercise equipment.

Daniel used barbells and a chin-up bar. A calendar hanging on the wall bore meticulous notes and figures. He kept track of how many sit-ups he did. Not many reps with the weights. How many chin-ups.

"He was organized."

"He surely was," Carwyn said. "But I don't see any kind of planner or diary other than the wall calendar." He looked at Phil. "He kept one, didn't he? A personal planner?"

"Oh yeah. I saw him write in it pretty regularly, but he'd have it in his backpack."

Brigid went to the small chest of drawers and opened the top drawer. Neatly folded underwear and—if the stacks were even—four pairs of boxers missing. She opened the next drawer. "Socks," she muttered. "Four pairs." The next drawer was T-shirts. Again, four missing if everything lined up, which she was guessing it did. The last drawer contained pants. "Only two pairs of pants, but setting that aside, I think it's safe to say that wherever Daniel was going, he expected to be gone for four days."

"Which means" —Carwyn's voice was grim— "whatever happened with Daniel and Lupe, something did not go according to plan."

CHAPTER EIGHT

"Where can you get to and back in four days?" Brigid asked Beatrice the next night as soon as the sun went down. She and Carwyn needed to head out of town. Though they'd made progress, Brigid had the odd feeling that Lupe was slipping farther away while they tracked down Daniel Siva.

Even though Daniel was their best lead.

Why did you follow this boy, Lupe? It wasn't your style.

"There and back in four days?" Beatrice mulled the question over while Brigid packed her things. "I mean, in California you can get nearly anywhere in a day, figure a couple of days to do... whatever they were supposed to do—"

"That part is still nagging at me," Brigid said. "What was this 'action'? And why the fuck did this young man think taking a seventeen-year-old girl along was a good idea?"

"Maybe she had information they needed? Or skills?"

"Skills? She was a student. A good student, but all the same—"

"She speaks Spanish," Beatrice said. "Of course, lots of people here do. That seems thin."

"There has to be something." Brigid wrapped a pair of shoes and stuffed them in her duffel bag. "Maybe she knew someone. Had some contact that was important." Brigid tossed her new handgun on top of the shoes. "You've been monitoring her phone?"

"It hasn't been turned on since I started tracking it," Beatrice said. "If her boyfriend was smart, he probably got her a burner."

Brigid slid her shoes on. "What about before?"

"Before what?"

"Can we get a log of her calls and texts before she went missing? That might give us an idea of why Daniel took her."

"Good idea. I'll look it up and email you." Beatrice reached over and handed Brigid her black leather jacket. "Good to see you. I miss you. Come back soon. I'm annoyed that you just got here and we're headed to New York tomorrow night. I wish I could stick around."

"Depending on how long your visit is, we might still be here when you get back. Also, Carwyn is attempting to borrow your driver's car, so I'm sure we won't be leaving the state without returning it."

"He's trying to borrow Zain's Bronco for the trip?"

"Oh, but that truck's deadly, isn't it?" Brigid grinned. "I can't blame the man."

"It's very hot. Zain redid it, and now I want a black Bronco, but I can't get one because I'd be copying him. It's a conundrum."

"We're heading over to María Estrada's house to meet

with her before we go to Daniel's mother's house in Palm Desert. We should be able to do both in one night."

"And where are you staying in Palm Desert? That whole area is a bit wild. Technically it's Ernesto's territory, but I can't say that he has a good handle on it. Until you get to Vegas, it's the Wild West."

"Understood." Brigid grimaced. "Honestly? We'll probably end up in a cave or something. You know Carwyn and security."

"Do you have camping gear?"

"No. Would Zain have some we could borrow?"

Beatrice nodded. "You may have to sleep in a cave all day, but that's no reason to be uncomfortable. You better think about feeding too. I know of one bar in Palm Springs, but... let's just say it's not as reputable as Gavin's establishments."

Brigid curled her lip. "Does it have willing donors I can pay for a meal?"

"Yes. It does have that."

"Then I'll manage." Some vampires felt comfortable feeding off unsuspecting humans and wiping their memories. For Brigid, it felt like a violation. She avoided that scenario unless she was desperate. If she was desperate... Well, a desperate vampire was a danger to everyone, wasn't she?

"We'll head to Huntington Park first and then the desert. I'll ring you when we get someplace safe before dawn."

"Good." Beatrice gave Brigid a hug. "Any decisions about going back to Dublin?"

"Not yet." Brigid shrugged. "I have time. Let's find this girl first and see what happens."

———

"SCANDALOUS," Carwyn muttered.

"What's that?"

He looked at Brigid, who was scrolling though the email Beatrice had sent her.

"Scandalous how much I had to pay Zain to borrow his truck."

She looked into the back. "But he gave us all this camping equipment too. Even a solar charger for the electronics. That's handy."

He wasn't going to tell her how much the Bronco cost. They could likely buy a vehicle for less than Zain was charging them to rent his.

"So a stop at María's to update her, then off to the desert?"

"Yes. I also want to search Lupe's room, see if there's any clue in there as to why Daniel might have taken her with him."

"He doesn't seem like the type to humor a girl because of a crush."

"No, the opposite if anything. So there had to be a reason that he took her." Brigid put her phone away. "You smell good."

The corner of his mouth turned up. "You're going to need to feed tonight."

"Yes."

"Should we go someplace before we leave LA?"

"No. I'll be lazy all night if I do that. I need to keep my edge until we finish with Daniel's mother."

Carwyn constantly worried that Brigid played her hunger too close to the edge. At over a thousand years old, he only had to feed a couple of times a month. Occasional blood exchanges with his mate and hunting trips in the wild sated his hunger, but Brigid was much younger.

"Are you sure?"

"Don't worry so much." She sounded amused. "I'm sure."

"Fair enough."

Half an hour later, they pulled up to a small, neatly kept home in Huntington Park. In the driveway was an economical sedan and a work truck with EMILIO'S ELECTRIC on the side.

"Looks like her family's here," Brigid said. "Did you meet them?"

"No." Carwyn frowned. "Just María. I hope this doesn't mean they've gotten bad news."

"I think they would have called us, don't you?" Brigid pushed the door open.

"Probably." He stepped down from the Bronco and walked to the front door, then rang the bell as Brigid hung back. "She knows I work with my wife. She'll be expecting you."

"I know."

The door opened and a barrel-chested man with salt-and-pepper hair stood behind the screen door. "Hey. You must be the detectives." He pushed open the screen door. "Come on in."

"Thank you," Carwyn said. "You must be Lupe's uncle. How are you?"

The man's accent and manner told Carwyn he was a native of Southern California. "I'm doing okay. Still worried, but María says you guys have some leads on where Lupe might be? I'm Emilio, by the way."

He held out his hand and both Carwyn and Brigid shook it.

"We have a good lead," Brigid said. "And we've identified the young man Lupe left with. I know it's probably not much comfort right now, but everyone who works with this young man speaks highly of him. Nothing about him so far leads us to think he's a predator."

Emilio visibly relaxed. "I know she's not a little girl anymore, but—"

"We never stop worrying about our children," Carwyn said. "No matter how old they are."

Emilio nodded. "Yeah."

Carwyn saw lines around the man's eyes and knew that what María had told him was correct. This man cared about Lupe like she was his own daughter.

"Is your whole family here?" Brigid asked. "I was hoping to speak to Lupe's cousins. Her mother said they were close."

"Yeah. Robert and Angie. Rob's a couple of years older than Lupe, but Angie and her are the same age." Emilio led them down a hall decorated with family pictures and framed Catholic prints. Everyone was gathered in the family room around a coffee table with a carafe and several mugs on the top.

"Carwyn." María rose and held out her hand. "Thank you for coming." She turned to Brigid. "You must be Missus..." She looked confused. "Carwyn? I'm sorry, I don't know—"

"Brigid Connor." Brigid smiled and held out her hand. "It's very nice to meet you, Mrs. Estrada."

"I made coffee." The woman began to pour, speaking softly in Spanish to the woman next to her who was obviously her sister.

"I'm Carmen," the woman said. "Lupe's aunt. These are my kids, Rob and Angie."

Two older teenagers sat slouched in the corner.

"Hey."

"Nice to meet you."

Neither of the teens looked happy to be there.

"Angie, can you tell Carwyn—"

"I already told everyone she did not tell me she was doing anything, okay?" The girl was immediately defensive. "I knew she had a thing for this guy, but he was totally not into her. Or anyone, I don't think. He thought she was a little kid. Ask Father Anthony."

Brigid's radar must have been shouting at her. "We know all that, Angie. What do we not know?"

Angie stared at her. Very carefully. Directly in the eyes. "Nothing."

Robert huffed and elbowed his sister. "This is fu— freaking ridiculous, Ang. Tell them. They're professionals."

A flurry of Spanish filled the air. Carmen yelling at her kids. María speaking to Carmen. Emilio walked over to his daughter and glared down at her.

"Enough." He held a hand out and the room went quiet. "Angela, this isn't some game. You tell these people what you know about Lupe or your life as you know it is over. No phone. No privileges. No car."

"Oh my God, Dad, I don't even—"

"Tell them!"

She threw her head back and groaned. "God, she's so stupid."

"Are you talking about Lupe?" María said. "Angie, what is going on?"

"There was this girl at the mission one night, okay? And she was telling all these stories about a place out like on the border or something. Like one of those detention centers. And she was saying all this bullshit about how they were keeping kids out there and it was this big secret and how she escaped. Lupe bought the whole thing. Like, I looked online. There's no detention center where this girl was saying, so she was lying about it."

Robert crossed his arms over his chest. "You know there've been reports that there are private contractors who are keeping migrant kids in hotels and stuff, right? Places that aren't official?"

Angie pouted. "No."

The room erupted in shouts, mostly in Spanish, which Carwyn didn't speak as fluently as he'd like, particularly when people were speaking over each other.

"Did Daniel know about these stories?" Brigid tried to speak over the chaos. "How old was this girl at the mission?"

Angie ignored her mother and her aunt and spoke directly to Brigid. "She was our age, I think. But she said there were a lot of little kids there too. Maybe a dozen or something? Ones that had been taken from their parents, you know? I think Lupe told Daniel about it because this detention center was supposedly out in the desert where he was from."

"That was the action," Carwyn said. "I'll bet you anything. They were going to go rescue those kids."

"By themselves?" María was frantic. "She could get arrested. She could get deported. Oh my God, what was she thinking?"

Emilio looked ten years older. "What can we do? We can't

call the police. There's no way they would actually try something like that, would they? A teenager and a twenty-year-old kid? They'd have to be crazy."

"I don't think Daniel Siva is as naive as Lupe is," Brigid said. "I very much doubt they'd try to take on immigration authorities by themselves."

"But Daniel was from the area," Carwyn said. "It's possible he planned something with friends. If he knew where this detention center was, there might have been a plan with others who would help them. He's participated in standoffs with the government before."

Carwyn wasn't going to tell Lupe's mother that the man had only packed for four days. Whatever plan Daniel and Lupe had, it hadn't gone according to schedule or they'd already be back in LA.

"We're heading out to Palm Desert right now," Brigid said. "María, we're going to find them. Just to be very cautious, do you know an immigration solicitor who might be able to help if Lupe has run into trouble?"

"Solicitor?"

"Attorney," Carwyn said. "An immigration lawyer who might be able to help."

"We hired one last year," Emilio said. "Trying to get María and Lupe documented. I'll call her in the morning." He walked across the living room and held out his hand to Carwyn. "Tell us what to do and we'll do it. Just please, find my niece."

CHAPTER NINE

The flashing lights of passing big rigs illuminated the darkness in the interior of the Bronco as Carwyn and Brigid drove out to the desert. It was nearly midnight as they approached Palm Springs, the odd neon oasis in the middle of the Mojave Desert, home to Hollywood stars, quirky eccentrics, and more than one vampire looking to exist on the edge of immortal authority.

"Beatrice said this area is mostly unaffiliated. Officially, this is all Ernesto's territory, but unofficially, he doesn't have much financial interest out here, so he mostly leaves it alone." Brigid peered up at the shadow of towering windmills as they exited the interstate highway and took the road south to the Coachella Valley. Palm Springs and a series of small cities dotted the landscape along Highway 111 like beads on a necklace. They passed through the palm-lined roads of Palm Springs and drove through the scattered green oases in Cathedral City and Rancho Mirage before they saw the signs for Palm Desert.

"You have Robin Siva's address, right?" Carwyn asked. "Tell me when to exit."

Brigid glanced up from her phone. "Are you ever going to relent and let Cara in the car with us?" Cara was the electronic assistant that Murphy had programmed to assist with the voice-activated Nocht system. "If we had Cara, we could simply input the address and—"

"Never." Carwyn gave her a fearsome scowl. "Computers have their place, but I'm not letting my brain go soft so I can save time looking at something on a map."

"I suppose I should be thankful you finally relented and started carrying a mobile phone."

"Still annoys me."

Brigid laughed. "Old man."

"Young bird."

She tilted her seat back and stared at his profile in the passing lights. "If I quit my job in Dublin, where would we live?"

"Anywhere," Carwyn said. "If you want to stay based there, we stay based there. But if we were here..." A slow smile spread across his face.

"Ah Jaysus, yer thinking about that plane, aren't you?"

Giovanni and Beatrice had inherited a converted cargo plane with a specially constructed compartment to transport vampire passengers. Amnis, their natural elemental energy, interfered with most conventional avionics, so an airplane built for vampires was the height of luxury.

"You know they wouldn't mind loaning it to us," Carwyn said. "Wouldn't it be nice to skip the lengthy sea voyages in the very ugly freighters?"

"I rather enjoy boats."

"Liar." He narrowed his eyes. "Don't pretend you enjoy it. You put up with it, same as I do. But a week in a converted hold to cross the Atlantic versus hours on a cargo plane?"

"Fine, that would be convenient. I can't deny that." She glanced at Carwyn. "I've no desire to be under Ernesto's aegis though. I know we could get an introduction, but—"

"We wouldn't have to be under Ernesto's aegis."

"If we're in Los Angeles, we can't avoid it." She looked at the shops as they drove through the city. Boutiques. Pool supplies. Day spas. "Plus it's too sunny here."

"You're a vampire, woman! You only go out at night."

She wrinkled her nose. "It's a question of attitude. You know what I'm talking about."

"Admittedly, the overly suntanned people do make me suspicious."

"And the juice! Why do Californians speak about juice as if it was food? It's not food; it's *juice*. There's something wrong with humans here."

"Is it a bit like blood to them? We drink for our primary sustenance. The food is secondary, isn't it?"

Brigid slapped her palm on her forehead. "Now you've put the phrase *human juice* in my head, and I'll never forgive you for it."

Carwyn burst out laughing and didn't stop until she yelled at him to turn left at a light.

"Human juice." He said it and cracked himself up again.

"Don't keep saying it! And turn right at the stop sign."

People in Los Angeles were too cheerful. Too... glossy. Brigid knew if she lived in LA, eventually a killing spree at a juice bar was bound to happen. "I don't know that I want to live in America, Carwyn. I like my country."

"So we stay in your country if that's what you want."

"But that's selfish of me, isn't it?" She watched him carefully. "It's not just me. You've lived there far longer than you would have on your own."

"Brigid, I can live anywhere and be happy. You're my home, not this place or that."

She had no words. She'd never met anyone who loved her as generously as Carwyn. She had a loving family, but nothing compared to him.

"If we weren't going to question someone about a missing teenager, I'd have you in the back of this Bronco on the side of the road."

Carwyn gave her the saddest puppy dog eyes she'd ever seen. "Sadly, that's not an option. It was one of Zain's conditions for renting the truck."

Brigid's mouth dropped open. "What a nerve on that one! As if he'd be able to tell."

"I do have a tendency to break things when I get excited. Remember your house in Dublin?"

"Oh, that's right. Forgot about that." She looked around at the pristine interior. "Best not try the car then."

ROBIN SIVA LIVED in a run-down town house complex that had seen better days. The intense desert sun had bleached the paint that trimmed the houses, and the desert landscaping was overgrown with straggling grass. They parked in front of the narrow two-story house that was listed as her address and waited to see if there was any movement.

"It's two in the morning. Should we try tomorrow night?" Carwyn asked.

"That puts us another day behind." Brigid weighed the pros and cons of waking Daniel's mother up. She'd be groggy and irritated. She'd also be caught off guard. "I say we knock at the front and take our chances. Worst case, she doesn't open the door and we have to come back tomorrow night."

"You're the boss," Carwyn said. "Lead the way."

They exited the Bronco and spotted a neighbor's light go on.

"Someone's a light sleeper," Carwyn muttered.

"Let's see if Mrs. Siva is."

They knocked on the door twice, rang and bell, and waited. A light went on upstairs. Brigid knocked on the door again.

Minutes later, the porch light flipped on and a voice came through the door. "What do you want?"

"Mrs. Siva, we're looking for Daniel. We're not the police."

The door cracked open, a chain dangling at eye level. "Daniel don't live here."

"I know that, but we need to ask you some questions about him. Has he contacted you recently? Do you recognize this girl?" Brigid held out a picture of Lupe. "Daniel was seen with her about a week ago and she's missing now. Her family hired us—"

"That stupid fucker." The chain slid back, and the woman opened the door. Though she probably wasn't more than fifty, the woman's face was deeply lined and her voice indicated chronic smoking. Her skin, like her son's, was a light bronze and her eyes were dark brown. She had a long braid that fell over one shoulder and steel-grey roots in her hair. "He ran off with a little girl?"

"She's seventeen, but we do believe they're together."

The woman huffed. "Here I thought he liked the older women. Go figure."

"Why would you say that?"

Robin Siva patted her robe pocket as if she was looking for cigarettes. "Just the people he used to hang out with. They was all older than him. And he was in high school then."

Brigid had so many thoughts, but she kept them to herself. "Mrs. Siva, have you seen Daniel in the past two weeks?"

"Nah." She sniffed. "You ask his sister? He lives by her in LA now."

"We don't have her phone number, so no."

"Well, I can give it to you." Robin rattled off a 909 area code number. "I don't think Daniel comes around here anymore. Probably not a good idea anyway, so I don't judge him none."

"Why wouldn't it be a good idea?" Carwyn asked the question before Brigid could.

"He made his enemies," Robin said. "Don't think they forget someone who steals their drugs and throws them in the river, you know?"

"He did that?"

Robin pressed her lips together. "Sure did. And then he takes off, and who are they coming around harassing? Me. That's who."

"I'm sorry to hear that."

"Yeah, if Daniel was back, he'd probably be hangin'

around them old crowd, you know? I don't think he'd come around here."

"Can you give us a name, Mrs. Siva?"

"No." She shook her head and started closing the door. "I don't want any trouble. That boy was trouble enough. Him and his sister. I done my job with them."

"If these people have bad intentions toward Daniel or this girl, we need to know. We can protect them."

"You think I care?" She cackled. "I'm not getting involved. Take off, and let me go back to bed."

The woman's casual dismissal tripped Brigid's temper. She braced her hand on the door and took a step forward. "I don't think you understand, Mrs. Siva. You are going to give me names and numbers if you have them. This isn't optional."

The woman sneered. "Who the fuck do you think—?"

Brigid's hand shot out and gripped Robin Siva by the neck. The woman's eyes clouded over and her mouth went slack.

"Names please," Brigid said firmly. "And numbers if you have them."

———

CARWYN WATCHED Brigid writing down the stream of numbers that Daniel's mother had spilled under the influence of amnis.

"Is it wrong that I find it sexy when you get rough with people you're questioning?"

"When they could be protecting criminals?" Brigid shook her head. "No. Not wrong."

"The bar she mentioned, Down West?"

"Yes?"

"It's a vampire place. I remember hearing about it years ago. Run by a Romanian with a curious kink for old Hollywood."

Brigid frowned. "Interesting. I wonder if that's the one Beatrice was talking about."

"I very much doubt Beatrice would have frequented this place. I honestly don't know about us going there, particularly when you haven't fed."

"Why? Don't they have donors?"

Carwyn nodded slowly. "They do."

"And are they paid? Proper, aboveboard, and all that?"

"Mostly."

Brigid frowned. "So what's the problem?"

"It doesn't strike you as odd that Daniel's old hangout was a vampire bar?"

"Carwyn, half the bars in Dublin are owned by immortals. We like being around intoxicated humans. There's no mystery there."

"Okay." He slammed his door closed. "I still say there's something suspicious about Daniel being a regular there."

"We'll show up, ask a few questions, and I can top up my tank. Sounds like a fortunate coincidence if you ask me."

"I'll have your back," Carwyn said. "No matter what."

Down West sat at the end of a strip mall on San Pablo Avenue in Palm Desert, a line of gangly palm trees marking the edges of the parking lot. Though it was past three in the morning, the fluorescent sign was still flickering red and gold.

As soon as Brigid exited the vehicle, she could scent the immortals in the area. There was a mass of them inside, mostly earth vampires if she was reading the energy correctly. A few wind vampires wouldn't surprise her, but they were always harder to detect because their amnis was so diffuse.

"None of your kind," Carwyn said with relief.

The relief was genuine. Fire vampires were a volatile lot, but fortunately they were rare. It was only because of their long friendship that Brigid and Giovanni could stand being around each other. And despite the deep bonds between her mate and Giovanni, Brigid and Carwyn stayed in the guest-house when they were visiting. Female fire vampires tended to be on a bit more even keel than male, but not by much. If she'd been male, even the strongest friendship wouldn't have allowed her and Giovanni to be at ease around each other.

They walked confidently to the black-tinted door, well aware that they were being observed.

"Sensing lots of your kind," Brigid said, slipping her hand into Carwyn's. "Maybe a few wind vampires?"

"Scarlet—that's the owner—she's a wind vampire, but she doesn't keep too many around her. I'm guessing the majority here will be earth or water."

"Water vampires in the desert?"

Carwyn shrugged. "All sorts pass through here."

"It looks like a strip mall."

He squeezed her hand. "Looks can be deceiving."

A few steps away from the door, a vampire with sunglasses and a pale, shaved head pushed the door open and nodded for them to go in.

"Welcome to Down West," he murmured. "Corner booth on the far left."

"Thank you." Carwyn kept his hand planted firmly at the small of Brigid's back, and she was grateful for it. As soon as they stepped inside, the heady smell of human blood hit her nostrils and made her fangs lengthen.

The club was painted a deep burgundy, the color of red wine. The walls were lined with curving booths that faced an empty dance floor, and tables were scattered across the room.

The tables were empty, but the booths were mainly occupied, some with vampires and humans, some with just humans.

As they walked, the women and men in the booths beckoned to them.

"I'm clean. No drugs, no alcohol," one woman said.

"I like couples," a slender young man murmured from the shadows. "I'd love to meet you both."

"*Ceart*," Brigid whispered in Irish. "So it's that kind of place."

"Rooms in back," Carwyn said. "If you want privacy."

"Nope." If she could have blushed, she would have. "That won't be necessary."

"Scarlet's in the corner," he said. "Don't let her see you uncomfortable."

Playing it cool Brigid could handle.

What took her by surprise was seeing Daniel Siva with his head in Scarlet the wind vampire's lap, looking for all the world like a well-kept cat as she stroked his head.

"Hello." Scarlet looked up and offered them a smile. "Welcome to Down West."

CHAPTER TEN

"**F**uck. Me."

She blurted it without thinking and Carwyn cursed under his breath.

That's not playing it cool, darling girl.

"Sorry," Brigid said. "Your human looks so much like an old friend of mine, it's uncanny."

Good recovery.

Scarlet let out a shimmering laugh. She was dressed in an evening gown fit for a film noir goddess, her pale ivory shoulders glowing against the dark velvet booths. Her hair was set in perfectly formed dark brown waves, and her mouth was painted deep red.

"Isn't he pretty?" Scarlet said. "I just got him back. He's been missing for a few years."

"I hate it when that happens."

Carwyn had only met the woman once before, and it had been nearly fifty years. He wondered if she remembered him.

"You are the priest with the flamboyant fashion sense."

Scarlet pointed at him. "It's been too long." She examined him with a practiced pout. "And no Hawaiian shirt?"

"Packed in the luggage of course, Scarlet." He nodded politely and kept his hand on Brigid's back. "It's been a long time. I'm actually not a priest anymore."

Her fangs fell and she leaned forward, placing her elbow on the edge of the table. "Is that so?"

"My mate and I are just passing through." He emphasized the word *mate*. "On our way to Las Vegas for a bit of a holiday. This is Brigid."

"Hello, Brigid." Scarlet's mouth curved into a coy smile. "I do love your scent. More than a few immortals start their party here at Down West. You're welcome to browse, of course. It's late, so many of our donors have already gone home with patrons, but the ones left will be even more eager to please." She bit her lower lip and drew a single drop of blood that she licked away with the tip of her tongue. "If you see anyone you like, you can arrange payment with my hostess, Laura." She started stroking Daniel's head again. "Rooms in back if you're looking for lodging."

"Your hospitality is appreciated," Carwyn said. "We'll look around."

"So nice to meet you." Brigid watched Daniel. "I don't suppose your pet—"

"No." She looked up and the smile was back. "I'm a bit territorial about him."

Brigid looked at Carwyn, then back to Scarlet. "I understand completely."

"Enjoy your night." A hand clad in multiple gemstones waved them away. "Do make yourself at home."

Carwyn led Brigid to one of the few empty booths as they

surveyed the variety of donors. When Carwyn spoke, it was in Irish. "This complicates things."

"He's not a drug addict." Brigid continued the conversation in Irish. "He's a bite addict."

When a vampire bit a human for feeding, it was common to flood their senses with a profound sense of peace and euphoria. It made the blood flow more easily and kept the humans still and happy.

But if bitten too often, humans could become addicted to the "high" that vampire amnis offered. More than one human had wasted away, waiting for the next immortal to bite him. Sometimes the craving overtook good sense. A human could only feed a vampire twice a month if they wanted to remain healthy. Anything more than that would steadily make the human sicker and sicker until they died from anemia.

Every now and then a vampire like Scarlet would keep a "pet" like Daniel, feeding on only a small taste every night like an appetizer while giving the human the euphoric reaction. For vampires who wanted to attach a human to their side, it could be very effective.

"So Daniel Siva is Scarlet's pet," Carwyn said. "If he's here, where the hell is Lupe?"

"That's what I'm worried about." Brigid was biting her lip. "We need to get him away—"

"She's not going to let him out of her sight," Carwyn said. "You saw how she reacted."

"But we're not going to find out anything about Lupe until we get Daniel away from her."

"So... how do you propose we do that?"

Brigid looked pained. "I don't suppose yer open to causing an international vampire incident?"

Carwyn rubbed his temple. "That seems like a profoundly bad idea."

"Then I don't know. I already tried to snack on the man," Brigid said. "You heard her. She's not sharing."

"What if we used you to cause a distraction?"

"If this involves me exploding—"

"Do you have a better idea? It's the only thing that might get us and him out of here without a giant fight. Fire vampires are volatile. If you distract the bar by exploding, I can abscond with our human friend without anyone being the wiser."

"Shite." She knew it was a good plan, but that didn't mean she had to be happy about it. "So are you going to provoke the fight or am I?"

"I think I better," Carwyn said. "That'll make it understandable when I drop out of sight. No one wants to deal with an explosive woman."

"I like this jacket," she said. "And I haven't exploded for years. Yer goin' to owe me. Big-time."

"I appreciate you always, darling girl." He rubbed his hands together. "Now, how shall we do this?"

"Wait." She raised a hand and caught the eye of the hostess. "Eat first. Fight later."

———

BRIGID SNARLED AND raised a hand to slap him, but he caught her wrist.

"Don't even think about it." His voice rumbled under the pulsing music of the club.

"You think you can accuse me of that and get away with it?"

Brigid was feeling... What was the American phrase? Full of piss and vinegar? She'd fed from the girl near the entrance of the club that had bragged of clean living, and Brigid had to admit a full belly of all-organic human blood really did hit the spot.

"Oh, I wasn't accusing" —Carwyn sneered— "I'm *telling* you. I don't share, Brigid."

"But you think I do?" She bared her fangs. "You think I don't see how you look at her? How you look at all of them?"

They were on their feet outside the booth, and every eye in the bar was on them.

Brigid could already feel her skin heating.

"You think I'm an eejit?" Carwyn said. "You think I don't see how it is?"

"Oh, and how is it?" She yelled, "Do tell me, Father!"

"You're half in love with him! Act like a lapdog. He says jump and you say 'How high, Your Majesty?'"

"Take it back!" She rose on her toes, and tendrils of smoke started curling around her. She heard shuffling and saw humans running for the exit as her eyesight turned red.

"You're gonna have to go fast," Carwyn yelled in Irish. "I think I see someone with a fire extinguisher."

"Kiss my arse, I hate those things!" she screamed back, also in Irish.

Carwyn let loose with a stream of unintelligible Welsh that Brigid had no hope of understanding. She yelled back, and the air started to crackle around her.

"Fire vampire!" someone yelled, and the entire bar erupted in chaos.

Brigid tried to keep the blast in a controlled perimeter, but as always, the fire unfurled outward, pushing flames away from her body and devouring anything in their path. The last thing she remembered seeing was Carwyn winking at her and mouthing "love you" as he flung himself backward and took shelter behind the bar.

———

COLD AIR BIT HER SKIN, glass rained down, and Brigid felt rain falling. She looked up out of a pile of rubble and saw the remains of Down West burning around her.

The rain wasn't rain but an errant spray from a broken sprinkler system. A pipe was bent and shooting water across the giant hole in the ceiling above the spot where Brigid was crouched.

She stood up, naked save for a half-burned boot and a single sleeve, and gingerly picked her way through the rubble. Before she could make it to the entrance, a cold hand curled around her neck and flung her back into a charred booth.

"What did you do to my bar?" Scarlet screamed. "Are you a fucking newborn?"

Brigid's fangs dropped, and her skin prickled. The fire crawling around her drew close, fluttering against her skin and teasing her senses.

Scarlet fell back, survival beating anger. "Just go. Go and do not ever come back here."

"Smart," Brigid whispered. "Where did he go?"

"The priest? I don't know. He took off. Now get out of here!"

Brigid walked through what remained of the black glass door leading out to the street. She was hanging on the edge of control. The temptation to spread her arms and let the fire take over was strong. She'd watch the immortals around her blacken and twist in the vortex of her heat, their bodies charring in the warm light of elemental fire. She could watch as the building behind her turned to ash and crumbled.

It would feel so good.

The fire inside only ever lived on the edge of Brigid's control. It swelled her veins and ignited her basest instincts. When the fire owned her, Brigid was every inch the monster humans saw in their nightmares.

She left the charred remains of Down West and turned right with no thought for her own nakedness or care for whatever eyes found her in the night.

A homeless man walking along Saint Padre Avenue stopped in his tracks, staring at her. He took the cigarette from his mouth and held it out with a trembling hand.

Yeah. That looked good. Brigid took the cigarette, lit it from her smoldering jacket, and took a drag as she continued down the sidewalk. "Thanks a million."

"You're welcome," the old man said. "Say, do you need some help, young lady?"

Brigid turned. "I'm grand, but thanks."

She realized she was putting on quite the show, but Carwyn had probably driven a good distance to get away from prying eyes, so she kept walking, grateful for the cloak of night. Luckily it was late. Other than a surprised coyote, she didn't encounter another creature until she heard the familiar rumble of the Bronco engine down a side street.

She took off her single shoe and the jacket sleeve, tossed

them in a nearby skip, and walked to the Bronco where her husband was holding out a blanket to wrap around her.

"Brilliant work as always, wife."

"What were you yelling at the end there?"

"Prayers to Saint Jude. You looked terrifying." He opened the car door for her. "Did you see Scarlet?"

"Yes."

"Do you think she suspects anything?"

"About him? No, it was pure chaos. It'll be a while before she realizes he's missing." She climbed in the car and saw Daniel Siva curled in the back seat. "If I had to kill my favorite jacket, at least the ploy worked."

"We need to get some food in him," Carwyn said. "Need to dry him out a bit and get him thinking straight. All he's done so far is ask when Scarlet is coming to get him."

"Fuck, he's well gone, isn't he?"

"He is. Also, the sun's up in an hour. We need to find an empty house or somewhere light safe that's secure enough for him too. In about an hour, we're both going to be dead to the world."

"Do you have my phone?" Brigid asked.

"Swiped if off you when you started to steam up."

"Good man. Give me a minute and I'll find us an empty safe house. I can't guarantee it'll be comfortable, but I *can* guarantee it'll be dark." Brigid still felt jittery and on edge. "Then I'm going to need a bit of your blood. I could use a little grounding."

"I'm yours." He held out his hand and squeezed hers as they drove out of Palm Desert. "But let's get safe first."

CHAPTER ELEVEN

"Hello?" The voice echoed down the hall. "I heard something. Helloooo?"

Brigid's eyes flickered open in the darkness. The walk-in closet had plush new carpeting with a thick rug pad. Lying on top of their sleeping bags and cuddled up to her mate, Brigid was far from uncomfortable.

A quick internet search the night before had given Brigid the address of a brand-new development on the edge of La Quinta. There was a news article in the paper about construction being halted since the builder had gone bankrupt, but pictures online showed four beautifully intact—and empty—model homes.

There were numerous reasons to dislike modern home construction in the United States. The McMansions cropping up across the American Southwest were far bigger than anyone needed, used non-native building materials, and were ecologically unfriendly. Plus they continued population booms in areas where the natural environment couldn't support human growth.

They did, however, have enormous and comfortable walk-in-closets and spacious garages.

Carwyn and Brigid had hidden the Bronco in the empty three-car garage and secured Daniel in one of the king-sized bathrooms on the second floor before they looked for light-safe spaces to hide in.

Brigid had to do some convincing if she didn't want to end up sleeping in a hole in the ground, but the walk-in closet in the main bedroom proved safe enough for Carwyn's stringent standards after they set up a variety of security measures, makeshift locks, and alarms that would wake him should anyone trespass.

"Hellooooo?" Daniel rattled the chain where they'd attached his handcuffs in the bathroom. "Hey! If you're really not going to hurt me, will you fucking *let me go?*"

Carwyn rolled over and threw one arm over her waist, snuggling closer as he let out a deep breath. "He's been like this for the past hour. I think he knows we're vampires."

"And yet he has no fear. Where did we go wrong?" She closed her eyes and reveled in the steady warmth at her back. "You smell good."

"Are you still hungry?"

"No, I'm fine. Feeling good actually. Are you going to need to hunt tonight?"

"I'll see what I can find. I'm not to the point where I'll eat anything, but I wouldn't pass up a bighorn sheep if I can find one."

"Mmm. Fuzzy." She nuzzled into his chest. "Is that why your chest is so hairy? All the wildlife?"

"That and my wife hates it when I wax."

Brigid cringed. "Don't even like thinking about it."

"Heeelloooooooo?"

She groaned. "I suppose we should wake up and let him stretch his legs."

Carwyn rolled up to sitting and muttered, "We gave him plenty of space in the bathroom and a variety of gas station sandwiches and bottled beverages. I don't know what he's complaining about."

"Not feeling very charitable, are we?"

Carwyn raised an eyebrow. "The girl is missing, and he was partying with vampires in Palm Desert. You'd better be the one to talk to him because I'm liable to snap his neck."

"Understood." She stood and stretched her arms up and out. Her muscles weren't tight. Her body didn't need to be warmed up. Whether she was sleeping or not, she kept a fairly even room temperature. Still, the stretching was habit and it felt good.

Before she walked out of the closet, she turned to her husband. "He's an addict. You know that, right? Just because it's vampires and not drugs doesn't make it any less an addiction."

Carwyn took a deep breath. "When you were at your worst, would you have abandoned a child who was depending on you?"

Brigid thought back to the haziest days when heroin controlled her life. "I don't know. I'd like to say I wouldn't, but I honestly don't know."

Carwyn frowned, then nodded slowly. "Okay."

It was so hard for someone who hadn't been there to understand the desperation, the justifications, the fear.

Brigid changed the subject. "Have you already talked to Beatrice tonight?"

"I called her as soon as I woke and asked if she'd seen anything on Lupe's mobile phone, but there was nothing." He drummed his fingers on his knee. "What are we at? Ten days?"

"I think so. She's got to have a burner." Brigid was praying she had a burner. She threw some clothes on, walked down to the bathroom where Daniel was making noise, and knocked. "Daniel, I'm coming in."

Brigid gave it a minute, then opened the door and saw Daniel Siva sitting with his back against the bathtub, his cuffed arms in front of him, the chain attached around the base of the toilet. He was pale and looked thin, but other than that, he was fine.

"Who are you?" he asked.

"Forget me," Brigid said. "Where is Lupe?"

His guilty eyes made Brigid's stomach drop.

"She's not home?"

"No, Daniel. She's not home."

His face drained of color. "I don't know."

"What do you mean, you don't know?" Brigid crouched down to eye level with him. "You took a seventeen-year-old girl away from her family and out to the desert to help you on some mad mission to break into a federal detention center. And now you don't know where she is?"

"I left her at the hotel, okay? She had plenty of money. She should have gotten a bus back to LA. Hell, with as much cash as I left with her, she could have taken a taxi back home." He ran a hand through his hair. "Fuck!"

"Daniel, why did you leave her at a hotel?"

"I went by my mother's house because I had some camping stuff there, okay? Where this detention center was, I figured we'd have to be camping, so I went there to get my stuff. And fucking Warren found me."

"Warren?"

"One of Scarlet's people."

"So Scarlet was watching your old house? You didn't think she'd know you'd come back to town?"

Daniel shrugged. "It's been three years. I thought she'd have given up looking for me by now."

Brigid crossed her legs and sat in the doorway. "That's not the way it is with our kind. We can get possessive. Territorial."

Daniel glanced at Brigid's mouth. "What are you planning to do with me?"

"I'm not going to bite you if that's what you're hoping." She couldn't help but feel sorry for the boy. He looked strung out and desperate. "You're going to tell us where the hotel is, where the detention center is, and what the plan was. I suspect Lupe thought she was going to go through with whatever you had planned without you."

The seriousness of the situation seemed to finally break through. "That's nuts. She's a kid. There's no way—"

"Does she seem like a flighty girl to you, Daniel? Someone unserious? Immature?"

His mouth settled into a line. "No."

"I suspect you and she both know what's happened in some of those detention centers, don't you? Sexual abuse. Physical abuse. Children disappearing with no record of where they went."

"I know all that. Why do you think we were going to—?"

"Why do you think she would have turned back when the stakes were so high?" Brigid stood up. "You had a plan. She was carrying it through because it was important. That's the kind of person she is. Does that surprise you?"

He swallowed hard. "I guess not."

"What was the plan?" Brigid asked. "What was the next step?"

"There's a place out in the desert," he said quietly. "Kind of a squatter's community. It's called Liberty Springs. People go there in the winter when it's not too hot. It's off the grid. Good place to disappear if you need to. I called some friends there, and they were going to help us get the kids out, get them someplace safe. The Springs is only a few miles from the place the girl was talking about."

"Did Lupe know this?"

"Yeah." He nodded. "I gave her the numbers out there, but that was just in case she got lost or something, you know? I didn't expect her to go out there on her own."

"Does she have a phone?"

"Yeah. One of mine."

Brigid walked over and hauled Daniel to his feet. "I need the phone number, I need the name of the hotel, and I need you to clean yourself up. Take a shower. Eat something. You're going to help us find Lupe and bring her home."

————

THEY PARKED in front of the Desert Dweller Motor Lodge, and Brigid was not pleased by how many giant trucks were parked along the curb. "It's a trucker hotel?"

Daniel was sitting in the back seat, freshly showered, having just downed a double hamburger and a large amount of cola. Brigid could tell by his scent he needed about a dozen more burgers and a lot more water before he'd even be approaching the healthy young man he'd been before Scarlet had ensnared him again.

"It's just a place. It's cheap and you can use cash and no one asks any questions, you know?"

"What room were you in?" Brigid was hoping beyond hope that they would knock on the door and find a frightened but safe Lupe still waiting for Daniel.

"207." He nodded toward the sprawling two-story building. "'Bout halfway down that side there."

Carwyn, who had remained mostly silent since they'd taken off, finally spoke. "Young man, you should pray that she's in that room waiting for you."

Daniel didn't say a word.

They approached the building, and Brigid kept her radar out for any immortal eyes. This was exactly the type of place an opportunistic vampire would look for a quick and easy meal, so it was entirely possible that Scarlet's people had spotted Daniel here and not at his mother's house as he suspected.

"Anything?" Brigid asked quietly.

"Nothing I'm picking up."

Carwyn's radar was far more attuned than hers in situations like this. She walked up the covered stairwell, pushing Daniel in front of her, and followed him until he came to the door of room 207.

He knocked.

Nothing.

Knocked again.

Dead silence.

"You smell anything?"

Carwyn shook his head. "Nothing. There's no human behind that door."

Brigid's heart sank. Dammit, damn, damn bollocks, and damn. "Okay, let's go to the front office."

Carwyn nodded toward Daniel. "Do you want to take him with us, or...?

"You know what?" Brigid glanced back at the young man, who looked like a sword was hanging over his neck. "Take him to the car. I'll talk to the front desk myself."

She ignored Carwyn and Daniel as they retreated to the Bronco and she walked to the office, which was fronted by a faded carport and a dusty green carpet on the sidewalk. She pushed open the door and heard the clang of bells as she entered the room.

There was a half-sleeping man in a white undershirt and a cowboy hat sitting in the lobby, propped near a corner television where reruns of a detective show buzzed in the background. Behind the desk, a tired, middle-aged woman with dark red hair and a stained blue T-shirt was texting on her phone. She glanced up when Brigid approached, then looked at her phone again.

"Welcome to the Desert Dweller," she said. "How can I help you? We got rooms tonight. Sixty bucks for a single."

"Greatly appreciate it—"

The woman looked up when she heard Brigid's accent.

"—but I'm hoping you can help me with something else." Brigid pulled Lupe's picture from her pocket.

The woman's face fell and her attention drifted to the television when Brigid didn't express interest in a room.

"I hate taking your time when you're busy." Brigid reached into her other pocket and pulled out her wallet. "If you could give me just a few minutes, that'd be lovely." She pulled out three crisp twenties, the same cash a room would cost her. "For your time."

"Oh." The woman sat up. "Okay, sure. What's up?" She glanced at the door behind Brigid. "You're not a cop, are you?"

"No." Brigid laughed ruefully. "But I am an investigator. I was hired by a mother in Los Angeles. I'm looking for her daughter who went missing last week." Brigid held up Lupe's picture. "She's seventeen. Thin, medium height. Has long dark hair, and someone told us—"

"I know her!" The woman's eyes lit up. "Dammit, I knew she was in some kind of trouble. You don't hang out here by yourself for three days for no reason, you know what I mean?"

"So you remember seeing her?"

"I sure do, and you put that money away." She shouted at the man in the corner. "Pop!"

The old man blinked. "What?"

"Remember that sweet little girl who was here last week? The one I had to threaten Tommy's balls over?"

The old man frowned. "She okay? I knew we shoulda called someone."

The woman looked at Brigid. "I'm Celeste, and I tried talking to her. I saw her two times, walking to the taco truck that pulls up at the gas station across the way." She pointed out the window toward a brightly lit food truck with Tacos in flashing letters.

"Anyway, I tried talking to her, but she was real shy. Wouldn't tell me why she was here. Just said she was with a friend and they were waiting to meet some other friends." Celeste shook her head. "I don't poke my nose into other people's business—you just don't do that in a place like this —but that girl was making all my alarm bells go off."

Pop cleared his throat in the corner. "You know, most of these guys on the road, they're good guys. But I heard stories of some truckers that'll keep girls in their trucks and they threaten them to keep them there." Pop shook his head. "I mean, it's just stories, but I hear them a lot, and they even had a program on the news about it a while back. That's the kinda thing that just gives ya nightmares, you know?"

"When was the last time you saw her?"

"She kept the room for three nights," Celeste said, "and then she was gone. Left at night or real early I think, because neither one of us saw her. Just poked my head in the room when she didn't answer for housekeeping, and all her stuff was gone. I worried, you know? Thought about calling someone, but who would I call?"

Brigid handed her a card with her mobile phone number on it. "Call me. If you see her again, you call me. You were nice to her?"

Celeste nodded. "I tried not to scare her, but I might have done it anyway. Didn't mean to, I was just worried."

"She might remember you if she gets in trouble. Might come back. If you see her, call me right away. I'm Brigid Connor. My name's on the back, and her mum hired me and my husband." Brigid wanted to scream. They'd been so close. "So about a week ago then? That was the last time you saw her?"

"That sounds right."

"Did she make any calls from the room?"

"I can look, but I don't think so. She hardly talked to me at all." Celeste frowned. "She did ask if I knew about some hot springs though. I wasn't sure which ones she was talking about. There are hot springs all over the desert, you know?"

"Hot springs?" Brigid asked. "Or *the* Springs? Like the place?"

Celeste's eyes went wide. "Oh, maybe so."

"Do you know the place I'm talking about?"

Celeste made a face. "I do, but I hope she didn't head down there. Rough people if you know what I mean."

"Right." Brigid turned toward the door. "If she calls or you see her, call me right away. I really appreciate it."

"I hope you find her!"

Brigid strode to the car, her boots kicking up dust as she approached the Bronco. She wrenched the door open and climbed inside. "She headed to the Springs. Probably called some of Daniel's friends. Might have hitchhiked, they might have come and gotten her, but that's where she was headed."

Carwyn looked over his shoulder at Daniel. "How far from here?"

"Maybe three hours?"

He started the car. "You point, I'll drive. Let's go."

CHAPTER TWELVE

The desert took on an eerie glow under a full moon. Carwyn, Brigid, and Daniel drove back out to the highway, cutting south at what looked like the last service station on earth. The roads grew narrower and the saguaro cacti grew taller. Joshua trees and prickly pear dotted the landscape, and tumbleweeds gusted across a road illuminated by blue-white halogen bulbs.

Carwyn watched the highway with half his attention and listened to Brigid with the other half. She was speaking with Beatrice, but he only got snippets of the conversation.

"...on the seventh? Yeah." She scribbled something in her ever-present notebook. "What did the records show about...? No, I don't think so. Oh aye, that makes sense if she's just exchanging numbers."

Carwyn took comfort in the fact that someone had been using the phone Daniel gave Lupe. If they could confirm it was Lupe making the calls, that would be better.

"Gerald Jorgenson," Brigid barked at Daniel. "Ring a bell?"

"Gerald?" Daniel looked confused. "That could maybe be Jitters? I think someone said his name was Jerry, but that could be short for Gerald, right?"

"Could be." She flipped the pages in her notebook. "She didn't make many calls, but that one was the day she left the hotel, and it was the longest call she made. Nearly ten minutes."

Carwyn spoke up. "Who's Jitters?"

"He's an old guy, but he's like the unofficial head of the Springs. Kinda. If people want to do something big, like invite a bunch of people in or have a concert, stuff like that? They ask him."

"And you gave Lupe his number?"

"Yeah." Daniel shrugged. "I figured if something happened to me—"

"Something did happen to you," Carwyn said. "And you told a defenseless seventeen-year-old to call an old man in the desert instead of going home?"

"Hey, Lupe is the one who planned this, okay? She came to me. She was determined."

"And seventeen-year-old kids always know the right thing to do?" Brigid looked over her shoulder. "You should have known better, Daniel. You're the adult."

"Dude, I didn't know that Scarlet was gonna find me. Or that you two would, for that matter. Do you know who Scarlet is? She's not just any vampire." Daniel uttered the words as if they were some kind of warning.

Carwyn laughed. "Boy, do you know who *we* are? I'm not worried about a grifter trying to make a bit of coin in the middle of nowhere."

"Who did Scarlet tell you she was?" Brigid asked.

117

His voice was subdued. "She told me—she told everyone —she was like the head person in charge of all of California, you know?"

Carwyn muttered, "Soft in the head."

"How's he to know?" Brigid was smiling. "Daniel, she was exaggerating to scare you. Scarlet isn't any kind of authority in California. Maybe in Palm Desert, but Don Ernesto Alvarez is the vampire lord of Southern California and a good stretch of Northern Mexico too. We know Ernesto. If he found out Scarlet was calling herself the VIC out there—"

"Vic?"

"V-I-C," Carwyn said, spelling it out. "Vampire In Charge. She's not the VIC, and saying she is would piss Ernesto off."

"But right now, let's focus on Jitters, shall we?" Brigid looked at Carwyn pointedly. "After all, Lupe is the priority, and the day she left the hotel, she called Jitters. Would he come pick her up?"

"From where the hotel is?" Daniel shook his head. "No way."

"A taxi?" Brigid asked. "How did she get out there?"

"Probably hitchhiked," Daniel said.

"You better pray she didn't." Carwyn kept his eyes on the road. In the distance, he saw a half-crooked sign. It was too far away to make out. "We still on the right track?"

"Yeah," Daniel said. "We're almost there."

As the sign came into view, Carwyn saw what it spelled out.

"Liberty Springs." Tacked on with a smaller board was a less faded sign.

THIS IS PUBLIC LAND.

STRANGERS WELCOME.

Troublemakers are not.

"Turn in past the big cottonwood." Daniel scooted forward from the back seat and began to point. "People are probably all in bed by now. It's midnight, you know?"

"Then you can wake them up," Brigid said. "And hope they can tell you where Lupe is."

Carwyn had a sneaking suspicion this was going to be another dead end, which bothered him. Brigid was usually the pessimist, not him. Something about this case was getting to him.

He maneuvered the Bronco over uneven dirt roads that led between multiple makeshift encampments. There were old trailers and tents. Lights strung up and potted plants resting in the cool night air. In the distance, there was a flickering light as if a fire was burning.

Daniel steered them away from the fire and toward a large compound in the center of the settlement. There were tarps stretched from an old metal-clad trailer to trees along the perimeter. A ring of cacti formed a fence around the compound, and a makeshift gate marked the entrance.

Next to the gate, beneath the stand of cottonwood trees, there was an old water pump and a concrete pad.

"Looks like they have water," Brigid said.

"The Springs sits on an aquifer," Daniel said. "That's what Jitters says. I think he's probably right because everyone drinks the water and it's good. No one gets sick."

Carwyn parked next to the water pump and turned the car off. He could already see lights flickering in the trailer. They walked through the gate, which squeaked loud in the midnight silence. A second later, the lights flipped on.

After the cool light of the moon, the artificial beam nearly blinded Carwyn.

"Daniel? That you?"

"Hey, Jitters." He stepped forward. "Sorry I didn't call."

The old man was clearly half-asleep. "What are you doing out here? You lose your keys?"

"I'm not staying here anymore," Daniel said. "Remember? I moved to be close to my sister."

The old man was standing on what passed for a porch, wearing an old T-shirt and boxers. His stringy white hair fell around his shoulders, and he looked—if Carwyn had to describe him—like a harmless old man who was maybe homeless or maybe just didn't care anymore.

"Bad idea." Jitters shook his head. "You being so close to LA. Too many drugs and nightlife. If I was you, I wouldn't move there."

"I already did." Daniel walked closer. "I been gone about two years, Jitters. Remember?"

Jitters rubbed his eyes. "What are you doing back here now?" He spied Brigid and Carwyn. "You all lookin' for a place to hide for a while? We're off the grid, so you're welcome. If you don't have a place to crash, there's the church for tonight and we can get you set up tomorrow with something better."

Brigid walked forward. "We appreciate that," she said. "I'm so sorry to wake you, but we're hoping you can help us."

Jitters chuckled a little. "Little lady, I'll be able to help you better in the morning when I had some coffee."

"What about if we got you some coffee now?" Carwyn asked.

Jitters kept smiling through missing teeth. "Well, I guess if you can't wait—"

"We're looking for Lupe Martínez," Brigid said. "Daniel gave her your number, and we have a record of her calling you last week. Do you remember her?"

Jitters scrunched up his face and waved them closer. "Course I remember that girl." He sighed. "Daniel, you can't keep telling outsiders about the Springs. It's going to attract the wrong kind of people." He opened his screen door, and it slammed shut behind him.

Daniel motioned them to follow him. "Jitters, I only told Lupe about this place 'cause we were trying to do something important. Something you'd like, you know?"

He flipped on a switch just inside the door, and overhead lights illuminated the narrow galley-style kitchen. To the right, a living area dominated the trailer. The extension that usually popped out on the side had been removed, and a large deck extended the space. There was no door separating the outside, just curtains, so the evening breeze swirled the air and kept the interior from feeling stuffy.

Carwyn wasn't usually comfortable walking around in trailers—he always bumped his head—but he followed the old human into the living area and sat in the chair where Daniel pointed.

The old man stretched out on the couch and lit a cigarette from a pack on the coffee table. "Lupe," he said. "*Guadalupe.* You know what that name means?"

"No." Brigid sat next to Carwyn.

"It's Spanish," Carwyn said. "More precisely, a mix of later Latin and Arabic that was common during the Moorish conquest of Spain. Wadi-lupe, the wolves' river."

Jitters's eyes lit up. "A man who knows what he's talking about."

"Why did you ask us about Lupe's name? Is she here?" Brigid asked. "If she's not here—"

"That little girl was askin' to bring in the wolves." Jitters shook his head. "I told her, you can stay here as long as you want if you need a place, but you gotta drop that nonsense. Hell, Didi got attached to her right away. Wanted her to stay."

"Didi's like the chef here," Daniel said quietly. "She has kind of a restaurant on the other side of the well."

Jitters took a draw on his cigarette. "Didi's the one who brought her into town."

Brigid leaned forward. "When?"

"About... five, six days ago? Your girl got lucky," Jitters said. "Someone gave her a ride out to Dillon's Corner, and Didi happened to be in town to get food. She was askin' about the Springs and Didi heard her."

"How did she know to get to Dillon's Corner?" Daniel asked.

"Well, she called me." Jitters sat up and rubbed the back of his neck. "But you know I don't like driving at night these days. My eyes and all. I told her if she could find a ride to the Corner, someone from the Springs could come pick her up." He looked up. "And they did, so it worked out."

"You just left a seventeen-year-old girl to find her way to a random petrol station in the middle of the desert on her own?" Brigid was nearly vibrating. "Did you even think about how she was supposed to get there? I don't think buses go out that far."

"She could hitch," Jitters said. "That's how a lot of people make it here. And walking."

Every time someone mentioned hitchhiking, Brigid groaned.

Carwyn wasn't interested in blame at this point. He had a sinking feeling that Lupe had already moved on from this place, which meant they were spinning their wheels again.

"Is she here?" he asked. "Is Lupe here right now?"

"No. She moved on about three days ago. Stayed here for a time, trying to convince people that you were coming. Some of your old buddies talked to her, trying to figure out what she was wanting to do, but she clammed up. Said she needed to wait for you."

"She didn't mention anything about an immigration detention center?" Brigid asked.

Jitters's eyebrows went up. "Nah. I'd remember that. Was that what she wanted to knock over?"

"Knock over?" She looked at Daniel.

"He means rob," he said. "Jitters, there were some kids being held by government people. Immigrant kids who'd been taken from their parents."

Jitters shook his head. "Fuck no. Nothing like that. Why would she even think we could help with an operation like that? The boys are good at blocking roads and maybe blowing up the odd piece of mining equipment sometimes. Breaking into a detention center? That's like, armed resistance, man. I don't think even Wash would be into something like that."

Carwyn looked at Daniel. "Who's Wash?"

"He's a crazy fucker," Jitters said. "That's who he is. And he hates the government something awful. The government and car salesmen."

"Car salesmen?" Brigid asked. "Why car salesmen?"

"Honestly, I'm not quite sure." Jitters took another drag on his cigarette. "The girl mentioned Wash's name, but I told her to avoid him. Not sure if she did or not. You know Wash is curious about new blood in the Springs."

Daniel at least had the sense to look embarrassed. "I thought I'd be here when she met him, so..."

And you would have completely forgotten Lupe existed if you'd been stuck to that vampire's hip any longer. Carwyn gave Daniel a derisive glare before he turned his attention back to Jitters. "Where did Lupe go? Did she say?"

The man shook his head. "I don't know. Didi might know, but no point in trying to wake her up at this hour."

Brigid frowned. "Why's that?"

Jitters looked at Daniel. "You explain it." He rolled over and pulled up a blanket. "I'm going to sleep. You want more help, I'll get you in the morning. Right now I'm old and I'm going back to sleep."

Daniel rose and walked Carwyn and Brigid to the door.

"Didi drinks a lot," Daniel said. "Mostly at night. So unless you grab her before she starts in, she's gonna be wasted or passed out until morning."

Brigid sighed in frustration. "So we're stuck out here until tomorrow night?"

"I can stay here." Daniel nodded down the narrow hallway. "There's a bedroom here, and I know Jitters won't mind me taking it, but you guys need like, the dark right? I don't know where, but maybe at the church—"

"Don't worry about us," Carwyn said. "We'll be fine. You keep your arse planted here until tomorrow night though. If you don't..." He dropped his voice. "That would be a very bad idea, Daniel Siva."

"I'm not going anywhere."

When he spoke, he looked far older than twenty years, and Carwyn was reminded that he'd been playing juice-box to an unethical vampire for the past week.

"Get some sleep," Carwyn said. "And eat some more if you can find food."

"I've got some beef jerky in the Bronco," Brigid said. "Eat that before you go to sleep, and we'll see you at nightfall tomorrow."

CHAPTER THIRTEEN

B rigid stared at the star-filled sky from the window Carwyn had cut in the cave where they would spend the day. He'd cover it before the sun rose, but in the meantime, Brigid was enjoying the view.

Carwyn was still puttering and fussing with the design of the space. He'd cleared out a cave roughly the size of a small trailer just by sinking his feet into the desert floor. Sometimes in the bustle of the city, she forgot how mind-bending her mate's power could be.

The earth loved Carwyn. When he manipulated the ground, there was no sense of struggle; it was as if he whispered to the earth and it danced for him.

He sank his feet in the ground, and as he stepped, the desert floor fled before his feet, walking down, down, down until the cool earth surrounded them and a comfortable-sized cave appeared dug into the desert floor.

Overhead, the earth was raw and rugged, but beneath her, it was packed down smooth. She spread their blankets and sleeping bags in the corner and tossed their duffel bags near the entrance.

She lay back on the rude bed, and as she did, a clear round portal appeared directly over her. "Look at that." She watched Carwyn walk around the cave, his hands molding the walls into a safe and secure haven. "What a nice hotel room this is."

"You know I prefer this to empty houses. Here, no one is going to find us."

"I know, but as much as I don't mind the cave sleeping, it would be a bit claustrophobic for the human."

"I suppose so." Carwyn lay down next to her and stretched an arm out to play with the soft ends of her hair. "You hardly scorched a bit this time."

Brigid touched the fine hairs behind her ear. "One of these days I'll master it like Giovanni has."

"I don't think he's ever figured out how to protect his hair either." Carwyn tugged Brigid's arm until she was splayed across his chest. "He can't keep it long no matter how Beatrice would have him grow it."

"Good to know it's not just me." She was starting to feel the tug of the morning. It was winter and the nights were long, which meant her body was completely out once the sun came up. Carwyn could rouse himself during the day if he needed to, but Brigid? She'd sleep through an assassination attempt, which was why Carwyn liked to keep her safe underground.

"What are you thinking?"

Brigid blinked her eyes open. "About Lupe?"

"Yes."

"I feel like... she's close, but she's not here."

"I call María every night, but so far no one in the family has heard from her."

"We know as of yesterday, someone was using the phone Daniel gave her, so that's comforting."

"As long as she's the one making the calls."

"We have no reason to think she's not." Brigid tilted his chin so she could see into his eyes. "What's wrong?"

"I don't have a good feeling about this one," Carwyn said. "Part of me is wishing we'd gone back to Dublin."

"Liar." She tapped his nose. "You don't wish that for anything."

"Fine, not Dublin, but not this job." He frowned. "I thought it would be an easy, satisfying little quest and you'd be happy and feel rewarded and think to yourself, 'My husband is so brilliant.'"

Brigid snorted.

"'*So* brilliant,'" Carwyn continued. "'And wouldn't you know? This was far more fun than coordinating security details for visiting vampires. Far more exhilarating than the day-to-day grind of protecting buildings and people and boxes of mobile phones.'"

"Yes, it was so exhilarating I should just keep doing what Carwyn wants me to do!" Brigid said. "And forget about asset protection and foreign-visitor protocols. I should go fight crime and rescue princesses with Carwyn like we're vampire superheroes."

His hand landed on her backside in an affectionate pat. "See? You've got it exactly."

She smiled. "You had it all planned out, didn't you?"

"Except it's a far harder case than I anticipated." He pursed his lips. "I blame Lupe of course."

"How dare she be so hard to find after she wasn't kidnapped," Brigid said. "She should have just waited in the hotel for us to come rescue her."

"It would be a lot more convenient. Instead of her trying to rescue herself—and a bunch of other people—on her own."

"Damn those self-rescuing princesses." Brigid shook her head. "I blame feminism and plucky animated heroines."

"As you should." He lifted her up and set her on top of his body, running his callused fingers up and down her back, over her bottom, pinching the back of her thigh as she squirmed. "Keep wiggling like that and your clothes are going to fall off."

"They'll just fall off?" She couldn't stop her laugh. "I've never heard that before."

"It's well known that this is a thing that can happen to young female fire vampires."

"Rather specific phenomenon then, isn't it?"

"It's true." His fingers slipped underneath her T-shirt, and in one smooth motion, she was topless. "See? Look at that; you kept wiggling."

She stretched her arms up and around his neck. "Whatever will I do without my shirt on?"

"I'm sure we'll figure something out." He ran his hands down the center of her back. "I'm so glad you don't wear those nasty brassieres."

"I barely have enough tits to fill one out."

"And yet they're the perfect size for my big mouth." Carwyn rolled the two of them over and began kissing down Brigid's body. "Astonishing."

Brigid closed her eyes and luxuriated in his attention. "You always get so horny after you've been digging."

"There's something about a hard night's work that gives me ideas."

"So we're just supposed to forget about the case, the missing girl, and the detention center until tomorrow night?"

He started unbuttoning her jeans. "If you haven't forgotten about them in the next ten minutes, darling girl, I'm going to consider it a personal failure."

———

THEY EMERGED from the earth at dusk and washed off as best they could with the water jug they'd bought in Palm Desert. Brigid called Beatrice to check on Lupe's phone and see if there was any activity.

"I was able to grab a location yesterday morning," Beatrice said. "Just a rough one. It looks like she's back in the Palm Desert, La Quinta area again."

"Okay. And she's still calling?"

"Short calls only. She's careful. No texting."

"Someone has to be helping her," Brigid said. "We found out they were going to try to rescue a group of kids from a detention center."

"As in a government detention center?"

"Kind of? It's government but run by contractors. Daniel said that the girl told Lupe they had the kids in this old military base or something, and one of the children had disappeared. That's why Lupe was determined to find them."

"This is a nightmare. Let us know if you need any help. We have contacts in the area."

"I'll let you know, but for now we're still trying to find her."

"Kind of impressive," Beatrice said. "She's accidentally avoiding two of the best investigators in the world right now."

"Sheer dumb luck and technical naivete?"

"Yeah." Why was it so hard to track Lupe? Probably because she wasn't following any of the rules of avoiding detection. She wasn't trying to stay hidden, she just was hidden.

"She's turning the phone on and off as she needs it," Brigid said. "Probably trying to save battery."

"Which makes it a pain in the ass to track too. Where are you right now?"

Brigid sat on the tailgate of the Bronco and looked at the lights of the Springs in the distance. "Some odd anarchist, counterculture, off-grid settlement in the middle of the desert. She was here three or four days ago."

"Let me know if you make any progress."

Carwyn emerged from the cave after settling the ground back into place.

"Will do," Brigid said. "I better go."

———

"YOU'D BE surprised who shows up out here." Didi was an older woman with silver-grey hair braided and tied on top of her head with a bandanna. She was thin and suntanned, her skin tight and freckled from exposure. Her arm muscles flexed as she stirred a large pot of what looked like a hearty chicken soup.

"People from the city come out for my food sometimes,"

she continued. "People from the Corner come a lot. And all the folks around here that don't want to cook. People just throw in what they can, you know? So I do all right. If there's a concert out here?" She smiled, and Brigid saw three teeth missing. "I clean up those nights. I always cook something big." Didi nodded to the giant glass jar filled with cash on the corner of her counter. "It's a lot of work, but I don't mind that. I love feeding people."

"Were you a chef?"

Didi shook her head. "Nothing that fancy. Used to cook on a ranch a long time ago, back when they were still running cattle up north."

"It smells amazing," Carwyn said. "I'd love a bowl when it's finished." He threw a twenty into the jar. "Jitters said you might know where Lupe had gone."

"Lupe?" Didi's eyes turned suspicious. "What do you want with her?"

Brigid said, "Her mother hired us to find her. She didn't tell anyone in the family she was leaving; she just disappeared."

Didi frowned. "She a runaway? Didn't strike me as no runaway."

"Her family isn't the trouble, if that's your meaning," Brigid said. "She followed a boy—"

"Daniel?" Didi smirked. "She asked about him a lot at first. How did I know him? Who did he hang with out here?" Didi shook her head. "That boy. He's got a good heart, but he's clueless about the girls. She'll be banging her head on a wall over that one."

"Did you direct her toward any of Daniel's friends? Someone mentioned the name Wash."

Didi scowled. "Nothing good comes from hanging with that man. He's always yelling about one thing or another. He right threw a fit when I bought my truck." She nodded toward a truck that had to have been twenty years old. "I told Lupe to stay away from Wash. Hell, I tried to get her to just stay here with me and cook. I'd have split the profits with her."

"Did she talk about what she was doing out here?" Brigid asked. "Did she mention a camp or a detention center or kids that needed help?"

"Nope." Didi kept stirring the soup and shaking her head. "Don't know nothing about that kind of thing."

"Are you sure?"

"She tried to talk to me, but I just told her I don't know nothin' about crossing borders or rescuin' people." Didi shook her head vigorously. "I figure you want to get people out of a situation like that, you gotta know how people get into it first. And I don't know nothin' about that."

Brigid backed off. It was clear that Didi didn't want to talk about the kids in the detention center. Lupe might have run into the same problem. Out here, everyone looked out for themselves. There wasn't much room for compassion when you were living on the burning edge of survival.

"Where did she go?" Brigid asked. "When she left, where did Lupe go? Did she ask you for a ride?"

"Now, I can't be gone for all day, like taking her back to Palm Desert like she wanted." Didi shrugged. "I got people to cook for. I took her back to the highway. Left her at the truck stop there. She said she had a friend coming to pick her up."

"A friend? Did she say who?"

Didi shook her head. "Nope. I didn't ask. She knew her

own mind. Seemed real sure of things, you know?"

"Thanks, Didi. Appreciate it."

Brigid left Carwyn with Didi and wandered out to the front of Didi's compound, which was a lot like Jitters's compound next door. An old trailer, a line of cactus, and lots of tarps and makeshift shade covers. What set Didi's apart was the large outdoor kitchen and the long picnic tables in front that someone had built from old lumber and car parts. There was also a line of signs pounded into the dirt that seemed to spell out the credo of Liberty Springs.

LIFE IS HARD. DON'T MAKE IT HARDER BY BEING AN ASSHOLE.

DON'T CURSE IN DIDI'S YARD.

MIND YOUR OWN BUSINESS, BUT ALWAYS HELP YOUR NEIGHBOR.

KNOW WHEN TO ASK FOR HELP.

SHARE. DEAD MEN DON'T NEED MONEY.

There was a hint of menace to most of the advice, but they were still solid guidelines. Half a dozen people were already lingering around the picnic tables, ready for whatever the old woman was cooking.

Brigid saw Daniel in the distance, talking to a rough-looking blond man with Jitters at his side. She wandered over, close enough to hear what the men were saying without being obvious.

"...told you I'm sorry."

"These two look like fuckin cops to me, Danny. You think anyone around here wants the cops around?"

"I don't think they're police." Jitters was speaking. "Have you heard their accents?"

"Well, maybe they're foreign police. Like Interpol or

something."

"I'm telling you" —it was Daniel again— "they're not cops. And Lupe's not here, so they're gonna move on, okay?"

"What was that whole thing about, Daniel? That girl seemed to think you had some kind of private army out here. What the fuck?"

"I don't know what I was thinking, okay?" The young man sounded chastened. "She just came to me and she knew... I mean she knew some stuff I'd told her, and she thought I would know how to help. And I was fucking pissed, Wash. From what that girl in LA said, I'm pretty sure they're keeping these kids out at Miller's Range, and then the girl said one of the little kids disappeared. Like a baby. I had to do something. I thought maybe Oso—"

"If they're at Miller's Range, you're looking at miles of military reinforcements and fences and all that shit. If it was more accessible, I'd maybe try to put some people together, but not even Oso could sneak people in or out of that. Unless you have like a fucking tunnel machine or a helicopter, you're not getting in there."

"I know."

"There are things we can do and things we can't. Know your fucking limits and don't start running your mouth off about shit you can't handle."

"I know that now, okay?"

Brigid walked back to find her husband. Miller's Range. Lupe was looking for a place called Miller's Range, Daniel didn't have any super rescue group, and Carwyn and Brigid were back to playing catch-up with a resourceful seventeen-year-old girl.

Again.

135

CHAPTER FOURTEEN

"Darling girl, those humans may have been stymied, but you *do* have a tunnel-boring machine." Carwyn spread his arms as he followed Brigid out to the edge of the Springs where they'd parked the Bronco. "Right here. Why wouldn't we go get the children?"

"Because we were hired to find Lupe. Not take on the US government, possibly causing an international incident. We were hired to find a girl and bring her home."

Carwyn had a feeling that clever Lupe Martínez was going to stay under the radar until she wanted to be found. Or until there was someone willing to help her finish the mission she'd committed herself to. "How much money does she have?"

"Daniel said he left her with three thousand dollars."

Carwyn frowned. "Where did he get that kind of money?"

"He said his savings." Brigid gave him a skeptical look. "I have my doubts."

"As do I." Carwyn unlocked the car and boosted Brigid

up. "So Lupe has resources, and obviously she's smart. If we go to the detention center, we might find her there."

"Beatrice said her phone pinged in the Palm Desert area."

Carwyn didn't know what to think. "If she's leaving this area, where the children are located, why would she go back to Palm Desert and not go home? That seems like she's going backward but only halfway."

Brigid was staring over the dashboard when Carwyn got in the driver's seat.

"What is it?"

"Something Didi just said." Brigid rubbed her stomach. "I need to feed."

"You've blown up the only vampire bar in the area. You might have to hunt."

"Fuck." Brigid curled her lip. "I hate that."

"Find someone obnoxious enough that it won't make you feel guilty," he said. "Or we can look for bighorns on the way back to the highway."

"Fur in blood..." Her face was bordering on green. "Blood banks?"

Carwyn wasn't pleased. "It'll do for a stopgap, just don't make a habit of it. Preserved blood is like fast food. It'll keep you fed, but it's shit for your health."

"Blood bank it is." She bent over. "Cramps."

"Brigid, you push things too close to the edge." He wanted to snarl. She'd fed from him last night, but she needed fresh blood, human blood. And he couldn't give it to her. "Might not be a good idea to take Daniel with us if you're this hungry."

"So we just leave him out here?"

Carwyn shrugged. "Why not? At least we'll know where he is if we need him again."

"That seems cruel, but at a level I'm fine with," Brigid said. "Let's go."

Carwyn started the Bronco and turned down the main drag of Liberty Springs. He could hear Daniel shouting in the background and saw him running after the Bronco as they pulled away.

"Is he going to be safe here?"

"I think he came here after he broke away from Scarlet the first time," Carwyn said. "So she clearly stays out of this territory for some reason. He'll be fine."

"Odd." Brigid closed her eyes, her arm still wrapped around her middle.

"Tell me what you were going to say before." Carwyn tried to distract her from the ache in her belly. "There was something Didi said?"

"What?" She opened her eyes. "Oh, what was it?"

"I asked why Lupe would go back to Palm Desert, and you remembered something Didi said."

"Right." Brigid took a deep breath and tried to straighten her torso. "Didi said Lupe had a friend coming to pick her up at the truck stop. Was very certain of it. I think she met someone in Palm Desert while she was there. Maybe she struck up a conversation. Maybe she went looking for answers. Maybe someone offered her advice."

"And you think whoever it was, they were in Palm Desert, so that's why she came back?"

"I'm thinking..." Brigid doubled up again. "I'm thinking the minute we finish at the blood bank, we need to get our next round of fast food."

"Fast food?"

"Yeah." Brigid sat up straight, her features strained. "I'm thinking tacos."

"Tacos?"

"Yes. Definitely tacos."

———

BRIGID EXITED the alley door of the blood bank in Palm Springs feeling full, really and truly topped up, for the first time in a week. "You want to know one definite benefit to life in Dublin?"

"Plentiful bars?" Carwyn was leaning against the Bronco, waiting for her.

"Yes." She stood on her tiptoes and kissed him full on the mouth, leaving a smear of blood on his lower lip. "Oops."

He curled his lip. "You can't taste the chemicals?"

"If I wasn't so hungry, I'm sure I would, but right now?" She closed her eyes and sighed. "No. I don't care; I'm not hungry anymore, and that's all I care about at the moment."

"Fair enough." They returned to the car and Carwyn started it. "Did you say something about tacos earlier?"

"I did. Head back to the hotel, but park across the street at the filling station." It had occurred to Brigid that the one place the hotel owner had mentioned Lupe going was the taco truck across the road. Strangers? Maybe. But most of those trucks were family affairs, many headed by mothers or grandmothers who might see a girl on her own and make a point of talking to her.

"Because you're craving tacos?"

Brigid turned to her husband. "We're in California. What else would we eat?"

"Surfers?" Carwyn asked. "Hikers. A mountain lion if we stumble on one?"

"Pretend you remember what it's like to be human," Brigid said. "Just for a bit."

"Fine." He put the car in gear and drove away from the blood bank. "So we're going back to the hotel to get tacos. How does this help us find a seventeen-year-old girl?"

"We were working on the assumption that Lupe didn't know anyone in Palm Desert."

"Except Beatrice said her phone pinged here."

"Exactly. So what if she got to know someone?"

"You think she might have made friends with whoever was running the taco truck?"

"She went more than once," Brigid said. "Why not?"

"I suppose it's as good a guess as any."

———

THE TACO TRUCK parked across the road from the Desert Dweller Motor Lodge wasn't open at one in the morning. The sign was turned off, but the lights in the truck were still dimly lit, and Carwyn saw someone moving around.

"You want to approach them on your own?" Carwyn knew his sheer size could be intimidating. More than once, he'd let Brigid take the lead.

"No, I think I want you there." She opened the car door and Carwyn followed her.

Brigid walked to the side of the taco truck and tapped on the window.

There was a woman inside with long dark hair pulled back into a single braid. She said something in Spanish that Carwyn couldn't catch and pointed to the sign in the window.

Cerrado.

Closed.

Brigid tapped again, and a man appeared from the back. He was wearing a white T-shirt under an open flannel, and he slid the window back with a crack.

"Don't want to be rude," he said, "but my wife told you we're closed."

"I don't want to order food."

The man glanced at her, then at Carwyn standing behind her. "If you're not looking for food, we're definitely closed."

Brigid flashed the picture of Lupe. "Do you recognize her?"

The man shrugged. "Nope."

Carwyn's voice boomed in the silent parking lot. "You didn't look at the picture."

The man turned carefully.

"You should look," Carwyn said. "She's seventeen. She left home with a twenty-year-old man. Her mother is worried sick and hired us to find her."

The man hunched down to look out the window. "She's seventeen?"

"Never been away from home. Never been on her own. Barely seventeen," Carwyn said.

The man looked at his wife and spoke in quiet, rapid-fire Spanish that Carwyn could barely pick up. The wife responded, clearly unhappy. Her arms were crossed over her chest. She knew Lupe, Carwyn was certain of it.

"She might have lied about her age," Brigid said. "Or

ELIZABETH HUNTER

maybe she didn't. We don't care. We're not with the police. We just want to find her and bring her home."

The woman bent down and spoke through the window. "What if she doesn't want to be found?"

Carwyn took a deep breath. Lupe was safe. This woman knew where she was. There was someone looking out for her. The girl was safe.

"We know yer keeping an eye on her." Brigid stepped closer. "And believe me, I'm incredibly grateful. The last thing I want is for her to be on her own. But what she's plannin'..."

Carwyn stepped forward. "She's a good girl with a big heart. And she's passionate about protecting people."

The couple exchanged glances.

"We know that," the man said.

"This thing she wants to do," Brigid said, "it could put her at risk. I don't know what she's told you, but—"

"Lupe's not staying with us," the woman said. "But we know where she is. She's safe."

"She's not going to be safe if she tries what we think she's going to try," Brigid said. "Please, consider that her mother is frightened to death. She knows about the detention center. She knows what Lupe wants to do."

The man stared at Brigid with hard eyes. Then he glanced at Carwyn. Back to Brigid. He stood up and said something quietly to his wife. She finally nodded.

He scribbled something on a piece of paper and handed it through the window. "I'm Ruben Vasquez. My wife is Melanie. Our address is on the paper. Meet us there tomorrow."

"Night," Brigid said. "We can't meet you until tomorrow night."

Ruben frowned. "Okay, so tomorrow night. Meet us there, and I'll try to get Lupe to come over."

Carwyn stepped closer. "You're sure she's safe?"

"Very sure." Ruben looked bored. "God, these women are gonna kill me."

Melanie snapped at him in Spanish as she closed the window. Carwyn couldn't stop the smile as he grabbed Brigid's hand and started back to the Bronco.

"Do you really think she's safe?" Brigid said. "I didn't understand what they were saying."

"She's at Melanie's grandmother's house," Carwyn said. "Or I'm pretty sure that's what she said. Either way, they know where she is. She found some good people to help her. I told you, a clever girl."

"A clever girl wouldn't have left home with a twenty-year-old vamp addict," Brigid mumbled.

She was falling into a mood, and the only way to get her out of it was to plunge into the ridiculous. Otherwise she'd brood all day.

"Don't be so harsh, love." He opened the Bronco door and helped her inside, patting her ass on the way. To be helpful. "Don't you remember how out of your wits you became when we were first in love?"

Brigid frowned. "Are you joking just now?"

"Stammering. Starry-eyed." He almost closed the door but paused before he shut it completely. "It was as if your brains just fell out of your head." He patted her cheek.

"Are you barking?" Brigid asked. "When was this period of mindless adoration supposed to have occurred? I don't remember it."

"Well, you wouldn't though, would you?" He offered her a

pitying look. "I mean, I can't blame you, Brigid. There are not many specimens of manhood as fine as me. And I should know, I'm over a thousand years old."

Her nostrils flared as she tried to stifle a laugh.

Yes! Success. Carwyn loved it.

"Is that so?" she asked. "A *thousand* years?"

"*Over* a thousand years."

"Bless me, I had no idea. I mean, I'd probably forgotten it when my brain fell right out of my head, you know."

She was playing with him, and nothing made Carwyn's blood move like his wife in a playful mood. He shut the car door and walked to the other side. Brigid was waiting, her lips pursed and an evil light in her eyes.

"So a thousand years, is it?"

"Over a thousand—"

"That's right, *over* a thousand years." Her accent was getting heavy and all her *th*'s were turning into *t*'s.

He wasn't a *thousand* years, but he was definitely a *tousand*.

"So all that time," she said. "It's a right miracle you can get the engine going."

Carwyn had already started the Bronco. "Pardon?"

"I mean, a tousand years! That's just a miracle you can... Let's just say that it's a right miracle you can *rise to the occasion* at such an advanced age."

He snorted and laughed at the same time. "Aye, well I was built to last."

"I can see that. But tell me, do ya know for sure that it's a question of quality build or might it be pure fossilization?"

"Evil." He laughed, reached across the cab, and pulled her

into a hard kiss. "Give me directions to that empty house, darling girl. I'll show you how fossilized I am."

CHAPTER FIFTEEN

Carwyn woke an hour before Brigid. Though the sun was still up, it was sneaking toward the horizon, and when he pushed open the door, he could see the slant of warm afternoon light crossing the bedroom where they were hiding.

It was a brilliant idea, model homes. Brigid always seemed to find the ones that were bankrupt or nearly so. They were never disturbed by estate agents or workmen. She'd employed the technique half a dozen times or so since she wasn't a fan of Carwyn's technique for hiding.

Which was digging a massive, comfy hole in the ground. He loved it. Brigid, not so much.

He watched the light move and soaked up the warmth of the upstairs bedroom. The air was still and the desert around them utterly silent. He heard the wind whipping overhead, but that was all.

Two itinerant nightwalkers in a human-run world.

Carwyn had secluded himself for hundreds of years in his various hideaways. The small church in North Wales, his son's home in the Lake District, his daughter's home in South America. He'd retreated from the world enough that the stings and agonies of mortality touched him lightly. Those aches that he came in contact with were more spiritual than carnal in nature.

Then he found Brigid.

For Brigid, everything in the world was a wrong to right. She'd been a victim—been the one needing rescuing—but once she came into her power and tamed the fire that had burst from her when she first woke as an immortal, she was a force of nature beyond the element she wielded.

There was no human agony that didn't touch her, no injustice that was too small to confront. Brigid was a fighter, which meant Carwyn had become one as well.

They couldn't walk away from what they'd learned about Lupe and Daniel. If they did, Brigid would never forgive herself despite what she might have fooled herself into thinking.

The sun slipped below the horizon, and Carwyn felt her stirring beside him. He gathered her in his arms and rested her cheek against his bare chest. He felt the second that human instinct took hold and her breath began again. The blood moved in her veins and her heart gave a slow thud.

He closed his eyes and trailed his fingers down her spine, up and down, coaxing her back to life from cold sleep. He hated the thought of Brigid being chilled, but she was—just as he was—from the time she fell into sleep until the moment she woke.

If he could, Carwyn would wrap her in tissue paper and place her on the nearest shelf. As fearsome and unconquerable as his mate was, he had to fight every protective instinct when she walked into danger. It was as if when God had given him this woman to love, the Almighty had plucked Carwyn's own heart from his chest, re-formed it into a delicate crystal, and placed it in Brigid's hand.

He held her and started singing, filling her mind with the sound and scent of him as she woke. She took a deep breath and stretched against him, her right arm sliding around his torso. She flexed her hand and gripped the muscles on his lower back.

"Carwyn." Her voice was rough.

"Hmmm."

"What is that song?"

"It's a very rude drinking song if you insist on knowing."

"Not Irish."

"No, it's Scottish."

She smiled against his skin. "The best drinking songs are."

"As you and Gavin know."

"We should go to Scotland for a visit," Brigid said. "Visit Tavish and Max and Cathy."

"That's an excellent idea. But we have something to finish here first."

Brigid looked up, and Carwyn didn't know what to make of her expression.

"What is it?" he asked.

"Why is it taking me so long to find this girl? Even now, when we've tracked down where she's staying, I'm half convinced she's going to slip away again and we'll be off on our wild-goose chase."

"She's a clever one, Miss Lupe Martínez."

Brigid sat up and leaned against the wall. "She's human.

She's seventeen. And she's never been away from home before. It's ridiculous that it's taken us this long to find her."

"I suppose that since she didn't know how to be evasive, she's taken us by surprise. The girl reminds me a little of you."

Brigid snorted. "Hardly."

"Think about it." He sat up and braced himself on the wall opposite her. "She's stubborn, holds the world on her shoulders, and has no fear. She's a lot like you, darling girl."

"I wouldn't have left home when I was her age. I was too afraid."

"You might have if a clever, handsome boy came along and convinced you that you could save the world."

"Bollocks," she muttered. "I was barely hanging on to my own sanity. I hardly had the time to entertain saving the world."

He grabbed her foot and tried to distract himself from the thin black chemise she wore by playing with her toes. He'd painted them a ridiculous neon green the week before. "I don't know," he said. "I think one of the best ways to hang on to sanity is focusing on any and all problems other than your own."

She narrowed her eyes. "Are you trying to say something?"

"I said what I said." He pinched her toe. "Take what you want and throw the rest in the bin."

"I'm not avoiding your idea to quit Dublin, Carwyn, I'm just thinking about it practically. Look how long it's taking me to find Lupe. Maybe I need the security of an organization if I'm going to be effective. Maybe I need the backup and the support."

"And maybe you could find those things in other places if you looked. I'm not entirely useless as a partner, am I?" He batted his eyelashes. "I know I'm not as pretty as Tom Dargin, but I do have a rough sort of charm, don't I?"

Brigid laughed. Tom Dargin was Murphy's oldest vampire son, and he'd been a bare-knuckle boxer and trainer in his human life. His face looked exactly as pretty as you'd expect a bare-knuckle boxer to look if they'd been turned into a vampire.

"Tom." She sighed. "Oh feck, I miss everyone."

Carwyn's heart sank, but he forced himself to rally. "If you want to go back to Dublin, then we go back to Dublin after this. But we have to see this through."

"And by seeing it through, you mean grabbing Lupe tonight, taking her back to her mother, and catching a freighter to Dublin?"

"Pause that." Carwyn crawled over to Brigid and looked her straight in the face. "You're not serious, are you?"

"We were hired to find the girl, not to take on the US government," Brigid said. "I've been thinking about it, and it's just not something we can do. Not right now, and not in Ernesto's territory. Who are we? We're nobodies here. We don't have any role or jurisdiction."

"It's the middle of the desert. No one has jurisdiction out here."

"We could start an international incident."

"Sounds lively to me. What's the problem?" He sat back on his heels. "Are you serious? You're going to leave those children in a detention facility?"

"Carwyn, we were hired to find Lupe. Taking those children out of the detention center is as mad as taking on the

Sokolovs in Russia. We still haven't figured that situation out, and you want us to make another enemy? You know we have limits."

"I don't. Not for this, Brigid." He frowned. "There's something else bothering you."

"There's not." She reached for a shirt. "Come on. Let's go get Lupe and get her home. Anything past that is not our job."

Carwyn watched her dress and strap on her weapons with incredulity. He'd known she was frustrated, but he wasn't expecting this.

No, there was something else going on.

He rose, reached for his duffel bag, and pulled out the least pungent shirt. Whatever they did next, he really hoped there was a laundry nearby.

———

THEY DROVE to the address Ruben had given them the night before as Brigid read from her email. "Beatrice did a background check on the taco-truck owners. Their names are Ruben and Melanie Ochoa. They're both from Covina originally but registered their food truck out here about three years ago. Both sets of parents are in Covina." Brigid skimmed the info. "I see. There's a grandmother here in Palm Desert. Paulina De Santos. Looks like she's Melanie's paternal grandmother. That must be why they moved out here. Her address is like two blocks from Melanie and Ruben's."

Carwyn parked the Bronco on the street of a quiet residential section of Palm Desert. There were no sprawling lawns or crystal-blue pools behind these houses, but there were tidy yards lined by careful fences and lots of work trucks in the driveway.

A dog barked in the yard next door, running back and forth along the chain-link fence, yapping at them. Lights went on in the house, and Carwyn could smell tortillas cooking.

"Smells good," he murmured.

"Do not start eating." Brigid scowled. "We're going to say hello, thank them for looking out for Lupe, and then take that girl back to her mother."

As if that was going to happen.

Carwyn didn't say anything. Let Brigid have her delusions. He knew enough about grandmothers to know they'd be eating tonight whether Brigid wanted to or not.

Carwyn knocked on the door and stood back. There was the sound of the bolt turning and then a short, wrinkled grandmother opened the door and waved them in. "You must be Meli's friends. She asked me to get the door. Come in. We've been cooking all day."

The scent of tortillas and something spicy followed her like a cloud. Carwyn's mouth watered. He could almost feel his fangs falling, the smell was so good.

He looked at Brigid over his shoulder and mouthed, *Please.*

She shook her head, but he knew she smelled it too. Her face wasn't quite as resolute as it had been in the car.

They walked past a room that had to have been the kitchen based on the smells and the chatter of two women behind the door. The old woman led them down a hallway filled with dozens of framed family pictures on each wall. There were pictures of babies and school photos tucked in the edge of nearly every framed picture.

"You're Melanie's grandmother?" Carwyn asked.

"I am."

"You have a beautiful family."

"Thank you." Her eyes wrinkled in the corner when she smiled. "My name is Paulina, but everyone calls me Grandma Lina."

"Grandma Lina, thank you for welcoming us." Brigid pointed over her shoulder to the room they'd passed. "You said Melanie is in the kitchen?"

"She is, but she wanted me to take you to the living room to wait with Ruben. Dinner isn't ready yet." Grandma Lina raised an eyebrow. "You're staying for dinner, aren't you?"

"Of course we are." Carwyn looked over his shoulder. "Such a generous invitation, how could we refuse?"

They could hear a television on in the room to their left. As they walked in, Ruben looked up and offered them a low-key head nod. "Hey, you guys made it." The man was being purposefully casual, but Carwyn spotted the signs of tension. Lines around the eyes. A tense jaw.

"We did," Carwyn said. "Smells amazing."

"Melanie invited her grandma over to make enchiladas. They're the best."

"I can't wait to try them," Brigid finally said. "Is it just us?"

Ruben's eyes flickered to Grandma Lina. "Another friend of Melanie's came over too. She's cool."

"Excellent." Carwyn noticed what Ruben was watching on the television. "Is it a playoff game?"

"American football," Ruben said. "You guys watch that over... wherever you're from?"

"My wife is Irish," Carwyn said. "I'm Welsh. And no, we watch the proper kind in Dublin, but a good match is a good match, isn't it?"

"Okay." Ruben shrugged. "Whatever. You know the rules?"

"Mostly. I've traveled quite a bit in the US."

They chatted about the game, and Carwyn watched Brigid from the corner of his eye. She had her attention fixed on the door, watching like a leopard lying in wait. A black-coated cat just waiting for prey to fall into her lap.

Was it wrong to be turned on by your wife when she was in full predator mode?

Whatever. Carwyn wasn't going to think about it too closely.

Grandma Lina left to get drinks, and Carwyn spoke quietly to Ruben.

"Is she here?"

"Yeah. Melanie just said you were some friends. She didn't tell Lupe her mom hired you." He shook his head. "I don't know about this. Meli's not happy. That girl could bolt, and then she's gonna be worried sick."

"Well, tell your wife that my wife doesn't lose people when she's tasked to find them."

"No offense, but your wife looks fucking scary right now," Ruben said quietly.

He spoke quietly enough that he thought Brigid wouldn't be able to hear, but she did. Carwyn caught the corner of her mouth turning up.

"Hey, Ruben?" An unfamiliar voice sounded a second before a girl walked into the room holding a plate. "Grandma Lina told me to bring you guys some wings before dinner."

Brigid stood, tucked her hands carefully in her jeans pockets, and subtly moved to block the doorway.

"Oh thanks." Ruben looked between Carwyn and Brigid, clearly confused. "Uh…"

"Thank you, Lupe." Carwyn took the plate from the girl and smiled. "It's very nice to meet you. I'm Carwyn; this is my wife Brigid." Should he wait? The girl was already growing suspicious. "Forgive us for interrupting dinner with your friends, but your mother sent us, Lupe. She's very, very worried."

CHAPTER SIXTEEN

Lupe's eyes went wide. "Oh shit."

Brigid moved closer to the door before Lupe could bolt. She looked like a runner.

Carwyn put both his hands up. "Please don't panic. I promise we really are from your mother. Here." He pulled a crumbled envelope from his pocket. "She wrote you this note. I'm sure you recognize her writing."

"Lupe." Ruben was on his feet too. "You know you need help. You can't do this by yourself."

The girl looked confused. She read the letter, looked at Ruben, back at the letter. "So... what? My mom sent you guys to help me?"

"Help you get home," Brigid said. "And that's all. You're seventeen. You've done amazingly well on your own, and you're obviously a great judge of character because Melanie and Ruben are good people, but—"

"I'm not going home without getting them out." Cold resolve entered her eyes. "Do you know how far I've come? I haven't seen Daniel in days. I did everything on my own. I went all the way down to Liberty Springs and they couldn't be bothered, so I came back here and Melanie, Grandma Lina, and I are figuring out a plan, okay?"

Ruben crossed his arms. "What the hell are you talking about?"

The look Lupe shot Ruben was pure teenager. It was a combination of "I'm not telling you" and "you wouldn't get it anyway" with a definite flavor of "ugh, you're so old."

Brigid remembered giving that exact same look to her foster parents. She now understood why it drove them so crazy.

"Lupe, I don't know what you think yer goin' to plan, but breaking into a federal immigrant detention center is not something that is in your future. Do Ruben and Melanie even know your status?"

Ruben's eyes went wide. "Holy shit, Lupe, do you not have papers? What are you thinking? You've been out here on your own with— *Do you fucking know how many immigration raids there are around here?* What were you thinking?"

Tears had started to leak down Lupe's cheeks, but the set of her jaw didn't waver for a second. Brigid heard Melanie and Grandma Lina come running when Ruben raised his voice.

Melanie burst into the room and ran to Lupe. "What is going on? Why are you yelling?"

Ruben pointed at Lupe. "Did you know she was undocumented?"

Melanie turned to Lupe with wide eyes. "Lupe, why didn't you tell me?"

"'Cause I knew you wouldn't help me!" Lupe yelled. "And it's not about me, okay? I'm safe and even if I get... deported, I have cousins in Mexico and grandparents there and I'll be fine! But these kids, they don't have anyone. No one, okay? They're little and they don't know where their parents are and no one is looking out for them. No one!"

Brigid would have had to be made of stone not to feel the ache of Lupe's words. It didn't change her mind. She wasn't made of stone, she'd just spent a long time in the world, knowing that horrible things happened and you couldn't fix all of them.

Grandma Lina walked to Lupe and put her hand on the girl's cheek. "Lupe, you didn't tell me. If you had—"

"Don't you guys get it?" The girl's tears ran freely. "How can I go home and eat my mom's food and sleep in my bed, knowing that these kids are out there? They have nothing, and bad things are gonna happen to them, okay? Bad things have already happened. Who is going to help them if I just go home?" She made a fist and rubbed her eyes. "I'm not a child. I thought Daniel cared. I thought he really cared about other people, but he just took off, so I don't know what to think now, but I know that I care. I care about them. If no one else cares, *I care*."

"I care too." Carwyn spoke softly. "Lupe, we all care, but you getting arrested for breaking into a federal detention center isn't going to help anyone."

"Why are you all so convinced I'm going to get caught?" Her cheeks were red. "Maybe I'm smarter than you think."

"We know you're smart," Ruben said. "But how the hell—"

"I have a plan." Her chin went up. "And I have the money."

She had a plan? Brigid racked her brain, trying to figure

out what Lupe was thinking. What plan could get her into an old military base with that many reinforcements? Not that it mattered, of course. She was going home that night. But what could she have been...

That little girl was askin' to bring in the wolves.

I figure, you want to get people out of a situation like that, you gotta know how people get into it first.

I thought maybe Oso—

...not even Oso could sneak people—

Everyone was talking at once. Grandma Lina and Ruben were arguing while Carwyn and Melanie were talking near the door. All the women had tears and all the men had tempers.

And Lupe was standing in the middle of all the yelling adults, her chin lifted, completely set on whatever scheme she'd cooked up.

Completely confident that it would work.

"Where'd you find a coyote willing to take you to Miller's Range?" Brigid asked.

The question snapped Lupe's attention to Brigid. Her chin lifted. "I don't know what you're talking about."

The room had fallen silent.

"Was it Daniel's friend Oso?" Brigid asked. "Or someone else?"

Lupe said nothing, and Grandma Lina and Melanie were suddenly silent.

"Yer smart, Lupe. Very smart. But trust me, the pool you just waded into is far deeper than you can possibly imagine. I know smugglers. In fact, I work for one of the best."

There was trafficking, then there was smuggling. Trafficking was wholly illegal and immoral. But smuggling...

ELIZABETH HUNTER

Well... in the vampire world, that was a bit more of a grey area. After all, Brigid had been smuggled into the US herself. She had a fake passport, and she never went through customs. If Brigid had to smuggle someone or something from Europe to the US, who would she call? The very man she worked for.

Illegal cigarettes. People trying to get from one place to the other as quietly as possible. To a smuggler, they were both cargo. And Brigid knew that the worst thing that could happen to a smuggler was losing a load of cargo.

"Did someone give you a name? A number?" Brigid walked closer. "How much did you give him? Or was it a her?"

The kind of coyote that Lupe needed wasn't a human trafficker. It wasn't the criminal people pictured when they watched the evening news. No, the smuggler Lupe needed thrived on reputation and connections. They might be a government official or even a border agent. They forged documents, hid people behind false walls, and bought temporary visas that looked perfectly legal even to the educated eye.

They did not want any of their cargo lost. They wanted people to arrive safe and sound because that was how they obtained repeat customers.

They were also very, very expensive.

"How much did you give him?" Brigid asked again.

"Enough," Lupe said. "He'll get the rest when the kids are out of detention. That's the way it works."

"You didn't have more than three thousand dollars." Brigid shook her head. "It wasn't enough. The coyote conned you."

The first crack in Lupe's confidence appeared. "What are you talking about?"

"I'm telling you that we found Daniel, so we know exactly how much money you had. Unless you came up with a sudden influx of cash, the money you gave... whoever it was you three ladies called, it wasn't enough. Even the full three thousand wouldn't be enough. How many kids?"

"Essi said there were eight kids and four teenagers there. Minus the one kid who disappeared."

"That much cargo out of a guarded installation?" Brigid shook her head. "I wouldn't touch it for less than thirty thousand."

"Holy shit," Melanie said. "That much?"

Lupe's knees gave out, and she sat on the recliner in front of the television. She put a hand over her mouth. "Oh my God."

Brigid could tell Lupe believed her even if the news was unpleasant.

"I'm sorry," Brigid said. "But this ends here. Yer not getting Melanie and Ruben involved in this. Yer not recruiting Grandma Lina. Yer going to get your things, Lupe. You are going home."

———

"SHE'S A GOOD KID." Carwyn walked out of the house and into the backyard where Brigid was craving a cigarette and something stronger.

"I know she is." Brigid crossed her arms over her chest. "But she's in over her head."

They were waiting in the backyard while Lupe talked with the Ochoas and Grandma Lina.

"She *is* in over her head, but she's not wrong," Carwyn said. "Those kids in the detention center need help."

"So now you want to take on the US government?" Brigid asked. "We talked about this, Carwyn. We both decided—"

"Actually, you decided." He put his hands on his hips, and she saw his jaw settle into his stubborn look. "You decided that we needed to get Lupe home and that was the end of it. But you didn't ask me."

"So you want to help these children?"

He cocked his head. "You don't?"

"Carwyn, we have no kind of immortal jurisdiction over this, and unless—"

"Is this because you blew up the bar here in town? Because you slipped up? You didn't even slip up; I prodded you until you exploded. That was not a failing—"

"No." Brigid felt her fangs drop. "It's not because of the bar."

"Because this is your kind of job. This is exactly the kind of thing you normally love doing. So I'm not sure—"

"And what if we fuck it up?" She brought her head up and gripped her hands behind her back. "We don't have any backup here. We don't have a VIC or a patron. We don't have any authority. If things go badly, we have no one to bail us out."

"We have the church, and don't underestimate their influence," Carwyn said. "Why on earth are you doubting yourself now, Brigid? When have we ever needed to call in the cavalry as they say around here?"

She frowned and began ticking cities off on her fingers. "Manchester. Uruguay. Munich. Ham—"

"Okay, yes, we often call in friends to help us... finesse certain situations. But we're not helpless out here either."

"We're not calling Giovanni and Beatrice."

"Why not?"

"For one thing, they're probably on their way to New York right now."

Carwyn's eyebrows went up. "Oh, that's right."

"And honestly? We can't keep telling humans about vampires, Carwyn. There's too many who know already."

"So we'll figure out a way to help these children without telling Lupe about vampires."

Brigid crossed her arms. "And how will you be doing that?"

Carwyn opened his mouth. Then closed it. "I will be... digging."

"Digging?"

"Didn't someone mention getting into Miller's Range with a tunnel-boring machine?"

Ah shit. That had been her, hadn't it? "One of Daniel's friends mentioned using a 'tunnel machine' to break in, yes."

He spread his arms. "And here I am. I can tunnel under the range before the operation, find a few scrappy compatriots to help us break into the facility, and get the kids out through the tunnel. No one will be wiser about where they went."

Brigid was still skeptical, but it might work. *Might.*

"And what are we supposed to do with all these children when we get them out?"

"We'll figure that out later, but you cannot argue that they're safe where they are, Brigid."

She couldn't deny him on that. "We can't do this by ourselves. We'd need..." She thought through a very basic plan. "At least half a dozen people to do anything."

"So we'll find six humans to help us. Try to think through this strange cloud of self-doubt that has suddenly descended on you, because these are not government agents, Brigid. These are contractors. The likelihood that they're as competent as actual federal agents is very slim. And you and I are far more skilled than the average federal agent."

She stared at his handsome, optimistic, resourceful, punchable face. Damn him, he was actually making sense.

"Say we do this," she started, "who are these scrappy compatriots you've clearly already thought of?"

Carwyn grinned, and Brigid knew she was doomed.

———

BRIGID WALKED BACK INTO the living room where Ruben was pacing near the door and Grandma Lina and Melanie were sitting on either side of Lupe on the couch. Lupe rose when she saw Brigid enter the room.

Brigid came to stand right in front of the girl, forcing her to meet her eyes. What she saw in Lupe's expression put the last nail in the idea of returning the girl to her mother that night and bidding this job farewell.

Utter, complete, stupid determination.

Brigid said, "If we take you home, yer going to find more money and run away again to help these kids as soon as you possibly can, aren't you?"

"Yes."

She felt a twitch starting around her left eye. "Fine. We'll help you. But you have to do exactly what we tell you to do, and you have to pay attention."

Lupe's eyes lit up. "Serious?"

"Dead serious," Brigid said. "As long as I have a guarantee that you are absolutely not going to run from us again."

"As long as you're going to help me get them out, I'll stay with you. I promise."

Brigid held her hand out to shake, warming it before Lupe could touch her skin. "It's a deal. Now go pack your things. We're headed back to Liberty Springs."

CHAPTER SEVENTEEN

The night wind cut a frozen chill through the Bronco as they drove south through the desert, and the moon shone off the snaking tar lines in the cracked asphalt leading to Liberty Springs.

Brigid was sitting in the back of the car, trying to talk to Lupe. "Daniel's friends," she started. "How many do you think there were in the Springs?"

Carwyn looked at the girl in the rearview mirror. Her body language was relaxed, but her eyes were still wary.

"It was really hard to tell in that place," Lupe said. "A lot of people keep to themselves. I mostly talked to Jitters and Didi, but only during the day because Didi drinks a lot. That place reminded me of the homeless camps in LA, but you know... different too."

"Where did you stay?"

"At Didi's. She has a spare couch in her trailer. It was pretty comfortable. She's not like the other people out there. She had like, a normal life and everything. She went out there after her husband and baby died."

Carwyn was surprised. "When was that?" Didi had to be in her sixties.

"A long time ago, I think. She only talks about it when she drinks a lot. But that's every night. She wasn't violent or anything, but she could be real grumpy. But I'm pretty sure she and her husband had a restaurant or something. That's why she's such a good cook."

Carwyn glanced over his shoulder. He was watching the two of them in the rearview mirror, trying to figure out if Brigid was softening to the idea of helping the immigrant children. As far as Carwyn could tell, she was still in interrogation mode.

He'd looked at a map of the area, and even leaving Daniel's friends out of the equation, Liberty Springs was surprisingly well-situated for an assault on Miller's Range, which was an old missile-testing site with a surprising amount of information about it published online. It seemed to be the center of several different conspiracy theories as well as antigovernment sentiment.

There were existing barracks in the middle of the base and a large building that could have been a mess hall visible online, along with a large warehouse-type building and a row of what appeared to be offices lining the side of the base that fronted the public road.

Quite a bit of speculation flew around the internet regarding the purpose of Miller's Range, whether it was still in use, and if so, what was it used for?

There was one particularly paranoid chap who ran a website called Miller's Watch. Watchdog_46 had been keeping track of the comings and goings of the range for over three years. It was roughly six months ago that black SUVs with no government markings whatsoever entered the site, were waved through by two servicemen, and followed by more vans, more trucks, and more SUVs. The range had been a hive of nonstop activity since.

It wasn't unheard of for the federal government to farm out detention centers to private companies, but in Carwyn's opinion, it was a dodgy practice. There was less accountability and a profit incentive to keep people locked up. What motivation would there be to find homes for the detained minors if the company made money on each child? It was a system ripe for corruption.

"If there are fences and guards and everything, how are you guys going to get in?" Lupe asked. "Do you, like, know government people or something?"

Brigid shot Carwyn a look that very clearly said *Now she asks?*

"We're going to get in the old-fashioned way," Carwyn said. "We're going to tunnel in."

"That can take months!"

"It won't," Brigid said. "We have a machine."

Lupe looked confused. "A digging machine?"

"Something like that."

"How do you know it works?" Lupe asked. "Won't they be able to hear it or something?"

Carwyn said, "We've used it before. It's highly reliable and very quiet. Never breaks down. One of Brigid's favorites actually. She loves getting her hands on it."

Brigid bit her lower lip. "Funny you say that," she said. "I was just thinking it was a minor miracle that the tunnel-boring machine operates at all considering how old it is."

"A well-built machine can last for decades. Centuries even."

"So you say." Brigid glanced at Lupe. "Ignore him. We'll be tunneling into the range; then I'll sneak through to get the lay of the place. It's not going to happen quickly, but it won't take forever either."

Lupe settled back in her seat and clamped her mouth shut. She looked out the window at the desert flying by in the moonlight.

"Moonlight." Carwyn hadn't even thought about that. The moon was nearly full tonight. It would be madness to try to break into Miller's Range with this much moonlight. They'd have to wait until the night gave them a little more cover before they could think about breaking the children out.

Timing was going to be everything.

———

THEY PULLED into Liberty Springs well after midnight, and only a few lights flickered in the sprawling settlement. One of those lights was Didi's, so they parked the car in front of the long picnic tables in front and walked Lupe up to the trailer.

"She showed me where she keeps her key." Lupe crouched down and looked under a large stone tortoise with a cactus growing off its back. "You can leave me here. You said you have a place to stay?"

"We do. Are you sure you'll be okay here?" Carwyn asked. "Do you want us to wait?"

"It's cool." She stood up with a key in her hand. "Didi will be pretty out of it, but I'll just go to the couch and crash."

Lupe rubbed her eyes. "I'm pretty tired. I'll see you tomorrow?"

"Not until the evening," Brigid said. "We have some details to take care of during the day. Digging things."

"Right." Lupe nodded. "Okay, I'll just hang out here and help Didi."

"And if anyone asks what you're doing here, just tell them that we brought you and we'll be back tomorrow night," Carwyn said. "Oh, and Daniel's here."

Lupe's cheeks went a little red. "Daniel Siva is here?"

"He is," Brigid said. "Maybe just... avoid him until we can figure out what the plan is. I don't want Daniel to do anything stupid."

Lupe pursed her lips. "Too late."

Carwyn gave her a wry smile. "Now you're getting it. Seriously, avoid Daniel tomorrow. If he tries to ask you a bunch of questions, just ignore him. Brigid and I will deal with him tomorrow night."

"Okay." She hiked the strap of her duffel bag up. "I don't even know what to say to him. I gave all his money to—"

"You did what you thought was the right thing after he left you at that inn," Carwyn said. "He's got nothing to complain about, does he? If he asks you where the money is, tell them you gave it to us to pay for supplies."

Lupe nodded. "Okay. Hopefully Didi will have some extra work for me to do tomorrow."

"And don't forget," Brigid said, "we'll be close. Just hang in there until tomorrow night."

THEY RETIRED to their previously dug cave. Carwyn usually filled in any dugouts as sizable as the one he'd previously created, but he'd had a sneaking suspicion that they might be back. He spotted the massive three-branched Joshua tree near the hill where he'd dug out their shelter and turned the truck toward it, trying to avoid as much brush as he could.

"She's going to be all right there back with the old woman, isn't she?" Brigid asked.

"Lupe?" Carwyn nodded. "I have a feeling that Didi is a softie. And that girl has a keen sense of people, that's for sure."

Brigid nodded. "Good judge of character. She's suspicious of me."

"You're a lethal predator even if she doesn't know that consciously."

"She has no fear of you whatsoever."

Carwyn grinned. "Of course she doesn't. I'm a lamb."

"Yer a master of disguise is what you are," she muttered. "Digging machine, my arse."

Carwyn stepped out of the Bronco and immediately took his shoes off. He loved the feel of the earth in the desert. There was ancient peace in the ground there, but also a vivid sense of life that always surprised him. The earth beneath his feet was old, but few creatures had trod it. Its energy was fresh, even invigorating, despite the cold, dry air.

He took a deep breath and let his amnis reach down deep in the soil, searching for the echoes of his previous work. "I love it here. Don't you feel refreshed?"

"I have to admit my amnis is quick here. The air is dry, so the fire comes easily." She reached in the Bronco for the small ice chest she'd stolen from the blood bank. "The fresh air makes me hungry though. I've been battling it since we left the highway at Dillon's Corner."

"You eat. I'll rebuild our tent."

"An excellent plan."

By the time dawn came, Carwyn was tucked into a comfortable den in the earth with Brigid at his side.

"Sleep." He felt her fighting it. "Let the day take you."

"Love you, big man," she mumbled.

He brushed her hair back and kissed her forehead. "And you're my world, darling girl."

———

THE NEXT NIGHT when they met with Daniel and Jitters, Brigid was like a snake who'd shrugged off her old skin. Her eyes flashed and her movements were sharp and elegant as she spread the map out on the pool table outside Jitters's trailer. She'd moved from finding a lost girl to coordinating an attack. She was in her element.

"Miller's Range is only five miles from here as the crow flies. In fact, some of the infrastructure you have here isn't from an old farm like Jitters thought. It's from a base that was planned out here after the Korean War. They were going to expand the range and enlarge it to include a proper Air Force base. They eventually decided to close it down, and the land reverted to public use."

"But Miller's Range is still military," Daniel said. "Technically."

"Not just technically," Brigid concurred. "Practically. It's military one hundred percent. When we break into it, we will be breaking into a military installation."

Jitters looked uncomfortable. "Daniel, you know I don't want no trouble here. We got a lot of people here in the Springs that are trying to lie low. Keep off the radar, so to speak. If you bring the military down on us—"

"He's not going to," Carwyn said. "They're not going to be able to trace the tunnel back to him or anyone in the Springs. When I'm done, there won't be a tunnel, so no one in Liberty Springs will have to worry about the government following them back here."

"And how on God's green earth you gonna build a tunnel like that without anyone knowing about it?"

"Leave that to me," Carwyn said.

Daniel looked between Carwyn and Brigid. He must have suspected that one of them was an earth vampire, but he said nothing.

"So why you telling us?" Jitters said.

"Because we're going to need help." Brigid turned to Daniel. "You thought some of your friends might be willing to help get these kids out."

"Yeah, it's not right." Daniel looked uncomfortable. "But I don't know about breaking into a military base or anything."

"Direct action," Brigid said. "Or was it all bullshit? To accept a system is to participate in it."

A voice came from the side door. "You told me you'd help."

Carwyn turned to see Lupe standing there. He'd heard her approaching but didn't know if she'd be comfortable showing her face. He should have known the girl was tougher than that.

"You told me," Lupe said again, "that you'd help. That you cared. That no one should live like a prisoner."

Daniel stood when he saw her, and Carwyn saw the deep shame on the boy's face. "Lupe, I'm sorry."

"I don't want to hear about you being sorry. I left home and made my mother so worried. I didn't even leave a note or anything because you said there wasn't time."

"The money—"

"I don't care about the money," she said. "The money didn't help anything in the end. Right now you have people standing in front of you, telling you they can help you rescue those kids, and you're not sure because it's on a military base?" Lupe was clearly disappointed. "I thought you were so brave, Daniel."

The young man was gutted. Carwyn watched as his insides wilted under her righteous anger.

Good. That was good. He needed to realize that talk was cheap.

"I'll help," Daniel said. "And so will Wash and Steven and Oso." He glanced at Brigid. "After all, it's practically in our backyard, and no one in Liberty Springs is supposed to ignore their neighbor if they need help."

"Good man." She patted his shoulder. "Let's spread a map out and call in your friends." Brigid glanced at Lupe. "Is there any way we might get some coffee? It's going to be a long night."

CHAPTER EIGHTEEN

Brigid, Carwyn, Daniel, and two men named Oso and Wash were standing around a pool table in Jitters's yard, staring at an old map spread out on the pool table. Four empty beer bottles held down the edges.

"What we need to determine tonight is where the best route for the tunnel is."

Oso looked at the map, back up at Carwyn, back to Brigid, then pointed to the red target marked on the map. "Did you not hear anything I just said?" He was, contrary to his name, a whip-thin man with a skinny black beard and a shaved head. His hands bore multiple tattoos that Brigid guessed were gang related, but his voice and manner were soft. "We can't dig a tunnel to get into Miller's Range. I mean, we could, but it would take months and months. Maybe a year."

"That's because you said you don't have equipment to do it," Carwyn said. "I'm telling you we do."

Jitters walked out of the trailer and wordlessly handed Brigid a beer. She looked down at the cold bottle in her hand and saw a Guinness.

"Thanks, Jitters." She took a drink of the dark stout and schooled her face when the bitterness hit her tongue. "That's very thoughtful."

"I do what I can." He nodded at the pool table. "They making any progress?"

"Not so far."

"What kind of equipment are you talking about?" Oso leaned on the pool table. "A boring machine or something? I know more than a little bit about tunnels, and man, I'm telling you there ain't anything that—"

"It's experimental," Brigid said. "From Europe. That's why we can't show you. Just trust that we have one, will you?" She pointed at Carwyn. "He's used it before, and it's about as tall and wide as he is. So the tunnel will be large enough for all of you and the kids to walk through." She pointed at the map. "Just tell us where to put it."

Oso, Wash, and Jerry looked at Jitters.

The old man walked over and leaned on the table. "Well... I suppose if you was looking for the most direct route, you'd want to start about here." He pointed to a spot roughly a mile from the fences. "But that's real visible."

"Where can the entrance be hidden?" Carwyn said. "We have to keep it out of sight."

"Then I guess it'll be here," Jitters said.

The point he indicated was nearly twice as far as the first. Damn.

"Unless," he continued, "you want to know about a way that's not on your maps and such. Might be a little trickier to get equipment there."

Carwyn crossed his arms over his chest. "I'm open to it. What do you have in mind?"

"Like I said, it's not on the map—probably 'cause it's part of the base. Outside the fences though. There's a canyon on this side of the range." He pointed to the north. "That's where they'd do bombing runs way back in the day."

"But you're sure it's outside the security fence?"

"It was inside until about twenty years ago. A big storm wiped out a bunch of the fence line and they decided to move it in. Canyon's still there though, along with an access road that goes about halfway down." Jitters's finger ran along what looked like a ridge. "There's a road that slopes down here, and if you keep following it, it leads to the northeast corner." He drew a line. "It's rough, but it's below the surface. You'd be digging up basically, so they won't see you. And you're only about a quarter mile from the fence line."

Brigid watched him. "How do you know about this?"

"Oh, when that base was abandoned in the sixties, they left a lot of equipment in that back corner." Jitters looked around his compound. "Used to be you could go in and buy scrap, parts, that sort of thing. Got quite a lot of building materials for this place that way. Not sure if it was strictly legal and all, but the guards there, they'd let you in if you had cash. I noticed the access road when it was still inside the fence line."

"Has anyone checked on it recently?" Brigid asked.

"I think so." Carwyn frowned. "I have a distinct feeling that Watchdog_46 knows about that road. The angle on some of his photographs would seem to match."

Daniel asked, "Who's Watchdog...?"

"Watchdog_46?" Carwyn asked. "He's the local conspiracy theorist. Believes in UFOs, men in black, faked moon landing, crazy things like that."

Brigid looked at Oso, Jitters, and Wash, who still hadn't spoken. They were staring at Carwyn as if he'd slapped their mother.

"Not that all those things are that far-fetched," Brigid quickly added. "After all, with all that security, they must be hiding something."

Solemn nods were Brigid's only response.

"So we tunnel in with Carwyn's... equipment." Brigid barely concealed her smile. "Then we do some poking around. I'll do that. Take a look at the guard situation, find where the kids are being kept. Check out the camera situation, things like that."

"I can help with that," Daniel said. "If you want."

Wash said, "Yeah, Daniel's quiet. He's real good at that sort of thing."

Brigid nodded. "Okay, but that's all. First night, we're in and out. Reconnaissance only."

"When do we get the kids?" Oso asked. "We gonna get them all at once?"

"That will all depend on what we find at the range. We don't know enough yet." Brigid shook her head. "We were only supposed to be getting one teenager, not a dozen little kids."

Daniel had the smarts to look guilty.

"Speaking of Lupe, here are the rules," Brigid said. "She is not going near any of this. I don't know if all of you know, but she's undocumented, which means if things in there go to shit and she's caught, she's in a lot more trouble than any of you lot."

Oso raised his hand. "I'm a citizen."

Wash raised his hand. "So am I."

"I know you are; that's why you're going to be with us. I've already done a background check on both of you."

Wash frowned and darted a look at Daniel. "Danny, you know about this?"

The young man shrugged. "She didn't ask me, dude. I guess she's gotta be careful with the kids, you know?"

"I don't care about your past drug convictions, Mr. Owens." Brigid glanced at Wash. "I care that you don't use again, especially around any of the children."

Oso was looking uncomfortable. "You don't even know my name."

"No, but I have a friend who was able to hack into the LAPD's system." She glanced at his arms. "Your tattoos are distinctive, Alfred."

Oso's nostrils flared, but he said nothing.

"I'm not interested in your pasts as long as you don't pose a danger to children, but let's not be naive, gentlemen." She looked around the table. "We all know that I can't take that for granted."

There was silence for some time until Jitters said, "That's understandable, Ms. Connor. Especially for little kids like this who are probably scared out of their minds. We gotta make sure we don't make them even more scared getting them outta there."

Wash said, "I can put together probably... six or seven people who can help. People who have seen some shit and done similar stuff. Maybe not with the government, but with labs and businesses and stuff. I'll vouch for them; Daniel can too."

"Breaking into research labs and freeing test animals isn't the same as a detention facility," Brigid said, "but as I can't afford to be picky at the moment, consider them on the team."

"Fuck! What kind of background check did you do?" Wash's mouth was gaping. "None of us was ever arrested by—"

"It wasn't a *legal* background check, Mr. Owens." Carwyn smiled a little. "We have different streams of information."

Oso was watching Brigid with narrowed eyes. "What the hell are you gonna do with these kids once we get them out?" he asked. "We're not social workers."

"If the child has a family member in the US, we contact that person. I don't care about their legal status, family is the best option. If they don't, then we find their people." Brigid looked around the table. "It's as simple and as complicated as that. We get the children out and return them to their families. And we don't quit until they're home."

———

LUPE WAS SITTING in the corner of Didi's yard, half-asleep in the corner of a broken couch and covered with a giant blue-and-black-plaid blanket. She looked exhausted.

The lingering smell of chili filled the air, reminding Brigid that good Irish stout wouldn't cut it and she needed to drink another pint before she went to sleep at dawn. The blood from the bank was satisfying, but it didn't last the way that fresh blood did and she couldn't deny it.

Brigid walked over and sat on the end of the couch. "Hey." She patted Lupe's leg. "Why don't you go to sleep?"

The girl yawned wide. "Did you come up with a plan?"

"We did. Or the beginnings of one anyway."

"What do I need to do?"

"Stay here and lie low," Brigid said. "Yer not goin' near that military base."

"But—"

"It's not up for discussion or debate," Brigid said. "We're here; we're gettin' the children. The cavalry has arrived. You, a minor with dubious immigration status and a bright future ahead of you, are not goin' to be taking part in any illegal activities."

Lupe looked at her from the corner of her eye. "You haven't thought this through."

"Oh, I'm sure we haven't. This is an idiotic plan from top to bottom. We're kidnapping children who have already been kidnapped once. We have no lawyers, no social workers. We're basically instigating an international incident."

Lupe bit the corner of her lip. "But they're not safe there. Otherwise there wouldn't have been anyone who was just gone like that girl said."

Brigid turned toward Lupe. "I believe you. I believe that girl. And if these children or this place had shown up in any court records, immigration files, or lawyers' briefs, I'd likely have told you to get a sign and picket the immigration office with your do-gooder friends from the church."

But the truth had been, when Brigid had given the name of the girl Lupe met in Los Angeles to Beatrice De Novo, preschool mom, water vampire, and resident computer hacker, Beatrice had been able to find *nothing*.

Nothing about a detention center at Miller's Range. Nothing about contractors using it. Nothing about unaccompanied minors being held in Southern California. According to Beatrice, no records of these children existed anywhere in the system.

That set off every alarm bell for Brigid.

Lupe said, "They're not in any records, are they?"

Brigid shook her head.

Lupe looked into the darkness surrounding Didi's compound. "You know, they call me illegal, but what they're doing is illegal too. I looked it up, and there're international laws about that stuff. So if I'm illegal, then they are too."

"Sounds like maybe you should be a lawyer when you grow up. Shove that law right up..." Brigid caught herself. "...in their faces. You know, just show them that law. Take 'em to court."

"Maybe." She kicked her legs under the blanket. "I just wish my mom could be a citizen. She knows more about America than like, anyone. She's seen *Hamilton* a million times and read the book about him and everything. She's reading one right now about George Washington. Plus she works superhard, and we don't take anything from anyone really. She wouldn't even go to a food bank at the church when she lost her job a few years ago."

"Your mother sounds like a very admirable person, Lupe."

"She works harder than anyone else I know. Way more than most legal people."

"You know, you should probably drop the whole legal and illegal people thing. Cigarettes are illegal. Drugs are illegal. People are not illegal."

Lupe frowned. "Cigarettes aren't illegal."

"I mean the kind that come on boats at night and don't go through customs, those are the illegal kind."

Lupe blinked. "Oh. I've never heard of that."

She patted the girl's leg. "Yer a lamb, but I'm oddly fond of you. I like how determined you are."

Lupe grabbed her hand. "If you don't let me go with you guys, the kids might get scared. If a bunch of scary-looking grown-ups in black—'cause I know you're gonna wear black —like, storm in and try to take them, they're gonna scream and cry a lot."

Brigid pursed her lips. "Fair point. I'll consider this information. Maybe we can make sure some of the people Wash and Daniel bring are women who can speak Spanish fluently." She looked at Lupe. "I'm assuming Spanish, but I shouldn't. What did the girl in LA speak?"

"Spanish. She was from Oaxaca, but she said some of the kids were from Central America and there was one from like Cuba or something."

"But all or mostly Spanish."

Lupe nodded.

"Okay, good girl." She looked at the tables where a few people still lingered, drinking beers and getting a little loud. "Are you still okay here?"

"Yeah, none of the people come inside the trailer. It's just me and Didi."

"And she's okay when she's wrecked?"

The girl frowned.

"Drunk I mean," Brigid said. "Hammered. Bollocksed. You get the idea."

Lupe nodded. "Yeah, she's okay. She's never mean or anything. Not to me."

"Okay. Carwyn and I will be working tomorrow again, getting the digging sorted out most likely. But I'll be back as soon as I can tomorrow night."

"Okay. I'll tell Didi she just missed you." Lupe smiled. "She was muttering something last night about you and Carwyn and the bleeping vampires. But, you know, she didn't say bleeping."

Brigid froze for a millisecond before she realized Lupe thought it was a joke. "Oh, because of all the black clothes I imagine?" She laughed with all her teeth. "Didi should talk to my aunt. She hated the black clothes when I was your age. Always wanted me to wear flowers and that shite."

Lupe shrugged. "I like bright colors mostly. Things that remind me of the sun."

"When we're not working, do you know what my husband wears?"

"Uh... sweatshirts? Basketball shorts?"

"Hawaiian shirts, the brighter the better."

Lupe giggled.

"I'm not havin' ya on, it's true." She motioned to her chest. "Neon green and orange flowers and pink and blue and all. It'll sear yer brain. He takes pride in it, no lie."

Lupe was fully laughing at that point. "You don't let him wear his Hawaiian shirts when you're working?"

"Jesus, Mary, and Joseph, can you imagine trying to keep a low profile with a mountain of a redheaded man built like a steam engine, taller than the front door, *and* fitted out in a hula-girl shirt?" Brigid shook her head. "Vacations and leisure time only, I'm afraid."

"Every time I see him now, I'm going to picture him in a Hawaiian shirt like my uncle wears in the summer. It'll make him a little less scary."

"Oh no, you can't be scared of *him*." Brigid shook her head. "He may be strong as an ox, but that man has the world's biggest heart. He's the one convinced me to take your case." Brigid winked. "How's it feel going from runaway to client?"

Lupe looked at her feet. "I can't pay you."

Brigid stood and looked at the girl. "You can pay us by listening, playing things smart, and then going home and apologizing like mad to your mother."

"What did you tell her yesterday?"

"Just that you were safe, you were staying with good people, but it was going to take a few more days to sort things out so you could come home."

Lupe's eyebrows rose. "And she was okay with that?"

"I have no idea—I made Carwyn call her. Mothers make me run screaming."

CHAPTER NINETEEN

They lay stretched on their bellies behind the rise of the ridge, looking through binoculars they'd borrowed from Didi, who liked to bird-watch.

"It's near midnight, and that's only the second patrol." Brigid passed the specs to Carwyn. "If this is military, it's sloppy."

"I told you it's not military," Carwyn said. "And in my experience, mercenaries—"

"Contractors."

"Mercenaries" —he shot her a side-eyed look— "don't have the organizational discipline that regulars do. These men are guarding children that no one knows about. They don't expect anyone to challenge them, so they're playing loose. If I had to bet, there will be one more patrol along the perimeter before dawn. Maximum two. These people will be easy to work around."

"Agreed. Are you picking up any sensors?" Brigid asked.

"No, but you might be better at sniffing those out."

Fire vampires were often attuned to currents of any kind.

Electrical fencing, bugs, and sensors were things that Brigid had trained herself to pick up.

"I'll give the perimeter a quick pass before I head back to the Springs," she said. "When are you going to start digging?"

"Tonight. I've identified the road that Jitters was talking about. It's well out of anyone's sight, and we both know I won't be visible for more than a minute or two. The real bonus will be that we can park a vehicle back there and no one will be able to see it unless they're in the air."

"Grand. So if you start tonight, you'll finish—"

"Tonight." He shot her a grin. "A leisurely walk in the park, this one is. The only thing softer than sandstone is lava rock. I'll officially finish tomorrow though. Don't want the humans getting suspicious."

"Once yer in, do you think you'll be able to get closer, see what kind of manpower we're talkin' about?"

"I want you to do a thorough sweep tomorrow night. You're better at picking up details, but I'll do a preliminary survey after I'm in." Carwyn rolled over and kissed her square on the mouth. "Have you eaten?"

She shook her head. "I've only got two more bags and I'm rationing them until I can get my fangs into some of your mercenaries."

"No stab of conscience for the sellouts, eh?"

Brigid narrowed her eyes and watched two tiny silhouettes move in the distance. "They're guarding kidnapped children. Possibly trafficking them if we believe Lupe's friend. These bastards will be lucky if I let them live."

"That's my girl." He frowned a little. "Still. Maybe have a pint tonight. I can feel your energy, and you're walking the edge."

Brigid rolled to the side and hooked her leg over Carwyn's thigh. "Maybe it's not human blood I'm craving." She reached down and ran her hand up the inside of her husband's thigh, tracing the line of his femoral artery to his groin. "Maybe I've been thinking of sweeter blood than that." She felt his body respond to her touch, the hard line of his cock growing beneath her hand.

Carwyn blinked and set the binoculars down. "Wife, are you trying to seduce me in the midst of a dangerous assignment as we surveil our enemy in the middle of the desert?"

Brigid nodded. "Yes, I am. If my estimate is correct, another patrol won't pass by this location for another three hours. And the time it'll take you to tunnel a quarter mile is far less than an hour. Even factoring in a generous margin of error, you have over an hour to kill waiting out here."

"You've calculated in a margin of error?"

"I wouldn't dream of neglecting that."

Carwyn reached for the bottom of her black T-shirt and tugged it over her head before he hauled Brigid over his body to straddle him. "I knew I married you for a reason."

———

THERE WERE no electronic sensors along the perimeter. The technology they were dealing with had stopped advancing in the seventies, maybe earlier. There was barbed wire and an electrified fence, but only in the areas easily accessible from the county road. She ran along the perimeter of Miller's Range twice, a blurred shadow in the darkness, before she started the extended run back to Liberty Springs, soaking in the damp air that had swept over the landscape in the past hour, leaving a flash of precipitation and the sweet smell of creosote.

The first time she'd come to the Mojave Desert had been to help a friend solve a murder. That had been years ago. Since then she'd dreamed of that smell, the unique bloom that only occurred in the American Southwest. It was just as she remembered. High on Carwyn's rich blood, she ran until the incendiary force that lived beneath her skin calmed to a manageable buzz.

Controlling the fire that lived in her was the work of eternity. Brigid would never be rid of the task. She would never cease being aware of the quick flash that could so easily spiral out of control, destroying anyone and anything around her that she held dear.

She thought of it when she was angry. She thought of it when she was excited. She thought of it when she made love. It was the constant drumbeat of her life.

Sex helped. Feeding helped. Feeding during sex helped the most, especially when it was sex with a grounded earth vampire.

Thank God Carwyn had a thousand years of pent-up sexual energy she could access nearly anytime she wanted.

Humidity also helped. So did ocean air. Fog. Any kind of balancing water element.

Like Murphy.

Yes, like Murphy. Her boss and his mate were both water vampires. So were Murphy's sons. So was most of their office. It wasn't intentional, it was just something that had happened for which Brigid was profoundly grateful.

It was also one of the reasons she was so attached to Ireland. The damp air that surrounded her nearly all year round felt like a cushion, a thin protective layer that helped to keep her in check. In the dry, crackling air of the desert, Brigid felt inches away from disaster.

She made it back to Liberty Springs, making sure to stop her run well out of town. She ambled toward the old Bronco, planning to leave the binoculars in the car and read her phone messages before she went to check on Lupe.

"I saw you running." Daniel stepped out from behind the Bronco.

The wind had hidden his scent from her, and Brigid stopped in her tracks, her fangs falling instinctively at the suggestion of a threat.

"It's not smart to sneak up on our kind." She shot him a look from the side of her eye and opened the Bronco door. "What can I do for you?"

He gulped, and Brigid recognized the look on his face before he even opened his mouth.

No, lad, don't do it.

Daniel stepped forward and raised his wrist to Brigid. "I know you're not a newborn. If you need to drink, I would trust you not to—"

"Are you really framing it like it's a favor to me?" Brigid shut the car door and leaned against it, carefully putting both her hands in her jacket pockets. "How much do you reckon Scarlet took before we came to get you, Danny?"

His face paled. "I know she took too much, but you're not Scarlet and I know—"

"Yer an addict." Brigid caught his eye and held it. "Like recognizes like."

Thoughts raced behind his eyes, a dozen questions before he managed to open his mouth. "I'm not—"

"You are addicted to the very intense dopamine rush that vampires use to lull their prey into compliance." Brigid looked into the distance, trying to make her words as impersonal as possible. "Some humans are more susceptible than others, and if you'd been working in a reputable club that only allowed a monthly or even biweekly draw, you'd likely never have gotten to this point, but there you are."

Danny's mouth fell open, but he didn't speak.

Brigid kept her voice soft. "How many times a week did she feed from you?"

"Ev—" Daniel cleared his throat. "Every night."

"That's not normal." Brigid shook her head. "That's not right. She took advantage of you. She probably would have left you a shell if we hadn't taken you from her."

"You don't get it. I wanted—"

"Course you did." Brigid stepped closer, still keeping a safe distance between herself and the vulnerable and appetizing human. "It's not your fault, lad. It's hers. She made you want the rush, and she only provided it when she fed from you. She's rewired your brain, and now—unfortunately—yer goin' to have to live with that."

His face screwed up in a flash of anger only to relax again. "You're saying I'm an addict. Like... a drug addict."

"Yes."

"And you said 'like recognizes like.'" He pressed his lips together. "What does that mean?"

Brigid resisted the urge to tell the human to fuck off and mind his own business. He'd come to her with a reasonable offer, and she'd opened this particular can of worms.

"It means that I'm a heroin addict," Brigid said evenly. "How do you think I died? Why do you think I turned into a fuckin' vampire firecracker? Died in fury. Sired in fury. I'm an addict for eternity now." She blinked, shoved the stab of pain to the back of her mind. "So believe me that I know what I'm talking about."

Daniel looked confused. "You're a *heroin* addict? But vampires—"

"Can't get high." She nodded. "I know. I could shoot as much heroin as I could find now, couldn't I? I could pump my body full of it and I'd never get the rush. Can you imagine that? I just feel the urge now. Just the *hunger*."

The realization of it began to grow in Daniel's eyes. "You're saying that I'm like that. That I'll always crave—"

"The bite? Sure you will. It feels good, doesn't it? Feels amazing. You'd be a fool not to crave it once you know what it feels like."

The young man's face was wan and hungry in the moonlight. "But I can have it sometimes, right? Just... didn't you say once a month I could—?"

"Do you think when I was human I could shoot up once a month?" She smiled a little. "You know what? I actually tried that. In fact, at the beginning I was very careful about self-medicating. Had a journal and a schedule and everything." Her smile turned bitter. "How long do you think I kept that up?"

"Not long?" His voice was barely audible.

"I was fooling myself. I didn't control it; it controlled me. I *was* an addict. I *am* an addict. I will *always* be an addict. Nothing changes that. Now instead of fighting the urge to get high, I fight the urge to let fire consume me and everyone around me."

Daniel went pale again. "Is that what happened at Scarlet's club?"

Brigid shrugged. "Everyone has setbacks, lad." She pushed away from the Bronco. "Put your wrist away. I'm not going to feed your habit, and I highly recommend you stay away from people who will."

They'd been walking in silence toward the distant lights of the Springs when Daniel asked in a hesitant voice, "Do you think Scarlet would have turned me? If I died, I mean. Do you think she would have turned me into a vampire?"

Brigid stopped and waited for him to turn toward her. "No." She made sure he understood the weight of her words. "I was turned by the foster mother who found me, the woman who had raised me since I was seven years old and who happened to be a vampire. She sired me because she loved me." Brigid took a breath and let it out slowly. "Do you think Scarlet loved you?"

Daniel looked at the ground. "No."

God, what a bitter pill to swallow. Brigid tried to soothe the sting the best she could. "Some of our kind aren't capable of love," she said. "It's not who they are, and it doesn't have anything to do with you." She waited for him to look up. "It doesn't have anything to do with you."

Daniel looked at her, looked back at the Springs, and started walking again.

Brigid walked silently next to him.

It was all she could do.

CHAPTER TWENTY

Carwyn felt a heaviness in his heart as he returned to Liberty Springs. The rage when he'd seen the children at a distance had flashed, then dulled. There wasn't much more he could do on his own, so he headed back to his mate. The tunnel was wide and the passage would be easy. He'd taken the time to account for little feet and tired legs.

They would need vans. The Bronco wouldn't carry all of them. They would need shelter and food. Blankets and hugs. As he approached his and Brigid's campsite near dawn, he felt the weariness hit him. It wasn't physical exhaustion—it was mental and emotional.

The crimes humans continued to commit against their own would never be understandable to him.

Brigid looked up from her perch on the hood of the Bronco, sensing his mood instantly. "What's wrong?"

He held out his arms and she ran to him. He took a deep breath, inhaling the familiar and comforting scent of her skin and hair. The subtle smokiness of her essence teased his senses.

"It's worse than we thought."

She looked up. "What do you mean?"

"There're more children. Lupe said the girl who escaped remembered about a dozen children there, but there are more."

"How many?"

"I didn't get too close, but from what I saw, closer to two dozen. And there are more men too. They showed up just after the third night patrol, an hour or two ago."

She nodded solemnly. "Okay, so we have to account for that. More children. More men. The basic plan hasn't changed though. We sneak the children out through the tunnel and—"

"I think Lupe needs to go with us."

Brigid didn't say a word.

"Think about it." He took her by the shoulders and looked her square in the face. "I'm a giant of a thing. You're a strange, foreign woman dressed in black. Daniel is a man. Oso and Wash are both men. These children are being held by people who look a hell of a lot like us. We need Lupe and maybe Didi to come with us."

"Lupe looks like everyone's big sister, so I get her, but Didi?"

"She speaks Spanish fluently and she doesn't look like she'd harm a soul. Can you think of a more perfect pair? We're not going to have time to win these children over, and if they're not cooperating, they'll alert the very people we're trying to avoid."

Brigid was shaking her head. "There has to be another way. Lupe—"

"Lupe is our best option," he said. "You know I'm telling the truth."

She knew it; she was just fighting it. "If anything happens to that girl, what do we tell María? What do we tell Carmen and Emilio?"

"We won't have to tell them anything because you're going to plan a perfect entry and exit." Carwyn squeezed her hand. "We'll go in tomorrow at dusk. You'll gather everything we need, and then night after next, we get them out."

———

THE FOLLOWING NIGHT, an hour after dusk, Brigid emerged from the tunnel, wearing stark black with her face painted to match her clothes. Carwyn hadn't taken that extra step, but then Brigid was planning to go much closer than he had the night before.

"Did you see any dogs?" she asked softly.

"No. What do you think of the tunnel?"

She nodded. "It'll work. The passage is wide enough not to scare them, the floor is smooth, and the slope should be manageable for the little ones."

"We can carry the smallest if we need to."

She stared at him. "How young are we talking about?"

"I don't know. A year? Year and a half?"

"Fucking hell." She was horrified. "They took babies from their mothers? Makes me want to kill them all."

"We can't focus on that now." He pulled her close for a fast kiss. "In and out, darling girl. Meet me here in fifteen."

A hint of a smile touched her lips. "Only fifteen?"

"Think you can do it?"

She was gone before he finished asking the question.

————

BRIGID KNEW the basic layout of Miller's Range from her perimeter surveys, but she resisted the urge to head to the dormitories where the children were being kept. Instead, she started at the gatehouse.

Where two men had been before, now there were six. Though it appeared only two were actually working, the other men did present an additional barrier to remaining undetected.

Unless...

They also presented an opportunity.

She moved in the darkness on the edge of the floodlights that lit the courtyard and spotted a half dozen black SUVs parked in a line near what looked like a hangar. She waited and watched, but there was no indication of movement from the building. She could hear people inside though. The air conditioner was humming, and a television was playing something with a laugh track.

She continued deeper into the old base, skirting cameras and avoiding lights. There was a mess hall with another television, this one tuned to cable news. Angry little men sat on safe soundstages thousands of miles from the California desert, railing against people they'd never seen in order to anger men and women they didn't know.

It was a game to those humans. The real suffering of others meant nothing to them. The anger made them money. Brigid turned in disgust but paused when she saw a tray of neat paper bags being rolled out the back of the mess hall, ushered by two men in dark battle dress uniforms. One was pushing the cart, and the other was armed to the teeth.

Brigid followed at a distance, noting the time the men moved.

7:07 p.m.

Was this the children's dinner? Did they not even eat together? They didn't receive a hot meal?

Disgusted all over again, she trailed the men until they arrived at a long row of what looked like dormitories. There was a low building in front with the remnants of a faded red cross attached to it. One by one, men who looked like soldiers arrived to carry the paper bags to the dormitories.

Brigid frantically counted the bags as they disappeared off the rolling cart. Ten. Thirteen. No, sixteen. No, twenty. In the end, twenty-three bags were taken off the cart and two remained.

Brigid was haunted by the two remaining bags as she moved closer to the dormitory. Who hadn't wanted to eat? Who wasn't able to eat? The bags were delivered. The men serving dinner left. And Brigid waited.

On the half hour, a man started a lazy circuit of the low building, holding an M16 on his shoulder as he walked.

One circuit around the building, then nothing.

Brigid waited far longer than the fifteen minutes Carwyn had teased her about. She waited to see a hand or a little face in the windows of the dormitories. She waited to see *anything*. There were windows next to each door, but the curtains inside them barely moved. A few swayed rhythmically as if they were being nudged by a fan, but for the most part, the curtains remained closed. The doors remained unopened.

On the hour, the man circuited the building again, looking for all the world as if he were patrolling a cemetery. He didn't look around. He showed no situational awareness. He simply walked, looked casually from side to side, and continued back to his chair next to the desk in the guardhouse.

Brigid was so tempted to move closer, but she continued around the back of the building and searched the outlying areas for any signs of life. There was nothing. While the front had been propped up, the rear of the base still looked mostly abandoned.

Which worked perfectly for her plan.

———

HE SAW her in the distance and knew she was as angry as he'd been the other night.

"Twenty-three," she said. "They're feeding twenty-three."

"Feeding?"

"I caught the tray with the bag meals on the way back to the dorms. There were twenty-five bags prepared, twenty-three delivered."

"They don't strike me as the type to spend money on extra food for the hell of it, so what happened to the other two?"

Her jaw was tight. "Good question."

"Twenty-three." He mulled over the number. "As long as they're old enough to walk, it's doable. More than we expected, but doable."

"I also have an idea to help at the front gate."

"I hope it doesn't involve you blowing yourself up,"

Carwyn said. "As much fun as that is to watch, we need you leading the rest of the team."

"I have no plans to blow myself up over these mercenaries," she said. "But it does leave me with an excellent idea of how Daniel and his friends might provide a distraction."

Alerted by a faint noise in the distance, Carwyn pulled Brigid behind him and dropped to the ground. He shoved both of them behind a rock and peeked out.

"What is it?" she whispered.

"Voices and lights." Carwyn watched the light come closer. "I'm not sure if it's one man or two."

"One would be idiotic."

"Well, there's no accounting for... Never mind, there are two."

"Two of them?"

"Coming directly toward us." He put his finger to his lips. "Tunnel?"

"I don't want them coming toward it."

"So let's not let them." He rolled the both of them toward another rise. "You know, if we made it fast and freaky, they'd never know we'd questioned them."

Brigid raised a brow. "Yer better at muddling brains than I am."

He grinned and wiggled his eyebrows. "Let's then. We might learn something useful." Carwyn scooted to the side and popped up, waving both his hands.

"Oi! Over here, boyos! I've got a wee question or two if you might."

"Carwyn, they might have radios!"

"Oh fuck." He rushed toward the men just as one was

taking out a communicator of some kind and knocked it out of his hand. "Forgot about that bit!"

He heard his wife muttering something dire as he grabbed both gobsmacked humans and knocked their heads together. "Oops, will you look at how clumsy I am? What a mess." He knocked them again. "Oh, lads. I'm too sorry. What was I thinking?"

"Who the hell are you?" One of the men was blinking and the other one had nearly fallen over.

Carwyn grasped both of them by the neck and let his amnis flood their senses. "Hello, boys. I am the angel of vengeance, and you are going to tell me everything that's happening in your little sleepaway camp."

The blinking man opened his mouth and frowned. "I... No. Can't. Employees of... Canyon Security Systems operate under a strip... strict NDA. So... we can't." The man blinked. "Sorry."

"Oh, look at the lamb. An NDA." He whispered over his shoulder, "Brigid, we're out of luck, they've both signed NDAs."

She snorted.

Carwyn squeezed the men's necks, just a little. "It's okay, you can tell me. Even with the NDA."

The off-balance man managed to raise his head. "Really. Can't."

"I'm sure you can." He pushed more amnis into them and saw their eyes cross. "Now boys, who are the children you're guarding here?"

"Cargo," one man muttered. "Selling... They're picking them up in two days."

"What day?" He shook them a little. "Friday?"

"Friday morning. They brought those girls in, the older ones. Whooooole group of them three nights ago. That's what they were waiting for."

"Waiting for what? Girls?" Carwyn's stomach turned.

"There's an agent. He grabs... I mean, you get what you get, right?"

"Oh, of course." Carwyn had no idea what they were talking about, but the dizzy one appeared to be ready to talk. "You get what you get."

"So we had the kids. 'Cause the ones... the illegals he caught, they had the little kids. That was all. And the guy..." The one man drifted off, closing his eyes.

Carwyn let up on the amnis a little. "What guy?"

"Buys the kids," the blinking man said. "The guy who buys the kids? He wanted some girls who were ready to work. You know, older ones but not too old. That kind."

"And that's what came in two nights ago? Some teenage girls?" Carwyn felt bile rising. He wanted to bash both the men's heads in, but that would be messy. And probably not the best idea.

"Crossing by themselves," Blinky said. "No parents at all. No one... They can't even trace them."

"What a find, you brave big men." He could crush their skulls in his hand, bury them in the canyon, and not a single soul would know what happened to them save him and Brigid.

If he did it, she'd forgive him. If he did it, she'd understand.

Not the job, Father.

The discipline of a thousand years steeled him. Carwyn leaned close to the men and whispered in their ears. "This is a dream. You had a dream. Your dinner made you sick. You threw up and you passed out. You and your friend both."

He dropped them on the ground, leaving them both tossing their guts. When they came back to awareness, they'd feel unwell, dizzy, and nauseated. That would give them enough cover for why they had a hole in their memory.

As for Carwyn and Brigid? He walked back toward the tunnel, holding his hand out for Brigid to grasp. "We don't have two nights," he said. "We have to move tomorrow."

CHAPTER TWENTY-ONE

Carwyn and Brigid stood around the pool table in front of Jitters's trailer with the map of Miller's Range spread in front of them. Carwyn had drawn in the tunnel, and Brigid had marked where each of the guard stations was.

Wash, Oso, and Daniel were all leaning eagerly over the map, nodding and murmuring to each other. Jitters stood in the corner with Lupe and Didi, who was chewing on her lip nervously.

"I don't want nothing to do with this." Her eyes were bloodshot, and she held a large cup of coffee between her wrinkled hands. "Jitters, I ain't got nothing to do with this."

Lupe put her hand on Didi's shoulder. "Please, Didi. You heard what Brigid said. There are twenty-three kids there, and they need us."

"Twenty-three kids I don't know nothin' about," she muttered. "I ain't got no cause to be messing with the government, girl. I steer clear of all that kind of business. I don't bother no one and no one bothers me."

"You helped me," Lupe said. "When I needed help, you

helped me. And now Carwyn and Brigid can help these kids. They don't deserve to be lost. They need to get back to their families."

"Can't we just report all these people to the police?" Didi asked. "I mean, if what they're doing is illegal, the police should help, right?"

Carwyn said, "Unfortunately, Didi, I think the first whiff of the government sniffing around and these kids will disappear."

"I thought these people was from the Army," Didi said. "Or immigration or something."

"No. At least not officially," Carwyn said. "Two days ago I called the attorney Lupe's family had contacted for her mother's case, and she called me back today. There is no mention of this detention center in government records. Whoever is here, they are not on the public payroll, though they obviously have some connections that are allowing them to kidnap children whose parents are detained by immigration authorities."

"Agents take bribes," Oso said. "Trust me, some of them are pretty cheap, and a lot of them have no morals at all. For the right amount of money, they won't ask any questions."

"They're able to use this base," Brigid added. "So they have some kind of federal official in their pocket or a federal connection, but these people are not from the government. We have a feeling that this operation is completely off the books. Which means that when we disrupt them, they're not going to call for backup. They don't have any."

Wash frowned. "Didn't you say they were Canyon Security or something like that?"

"We just found that out tonight," Brigid said. "We've

already left a message at the attorney's office and have people looking into the company, but we don't have time to wait. According to the source we have inside, the kids are getting moved out Friday morning."

"That's like two days away," Daniel said. "I'm supposed to get a crowd at that gate in a day? I don't have time to—"

"You'll have to work with what you have because we don't have any options at this point," Brigid said. "You're going to have to get very creative very quickly because we need a big enough distraction at that gate to get twenty-three kids of various ages half a mile to this tunnel." She pointed at the corner past the boneyard where the wrecks of various military vehicles sat rusting.

Wash started nodding. "We can do it. We'll figure something out."

Oso was rubbing his chin. "I got some ideas, man. But aren't you gonna need some more people inside the fence?"

"Lupe and Didi are going with us," Carwyn and Brigid said. "We're a little bit afraid that the children won't react to men well."

Wash scowled. "Fucking assholes. I got a few other friends—female ones—who already said they're willing to help. Couple of them live in the Springs even." Wash looked at Didi. "Miss Didi, if Ronnie and Crystal said they'd come with you, would you be less nervous?"

The names seemed to relax Didi. "I guess a little." She looked at Lupe. "They're good girls. A little rough, but they're good people."

"I think I remember them." Lupe rubbed Didi's back, keeping her arm around the nervous woman.

"We don't know how many little legs we're going to be

carrying," Brigid said. "We only know there are twenty-three children being held. According to the girl Lupe spoke to in Los Angeles, around six of them are older teenagers, and the new arrivals are likely to be older girls as well." She pointed to the road that Carwyn had drawn in. "Jitters will be waiting with his big truck, and we can pile everyone in the back. From there, we come back to the Springs and load the children into various vehicles. We don't want them all together."

"And after that?" Jitters asked. "What are you going to do with all those kids?"

"That's a question for another night," Carwyn said. "For tonight" —he clapped his hands together and looked at Wash and Oso— "let's talk about explosives, shall we?"

———

"THIS WOULD ALL BE *SO* MUCH EASIER if everyone knew we were vampires," Carwyn muttered under his breath. "We wouldn't have to worry about the guards or the little ones or—"

"I keep telling you we can't let that secret out." Brigid was tucked under Carwyn's outstretched arm, examining the haphazard team they'd thrown together in a matter of hours. "It spoils our air of mystery, and also, do you really want to have to wipe the memories of two dozen children?"

"I suppose not."

They were sitting on an old couch in a corner of Didi's yard as Jitters went over a few of the finer points of dynamite with three wide-eyed young men. Lupe was sitting around a firepit with Didi and the two women Wash had recommended, Ronnie and Crystal.

Ronnie was tall, painfully thin, and looked like she'd had a rough life judging by the scars Brigid had spotted on her arms. Crystal was a salt-of-the-earth type, sturdy-built and square-faced. Her short hair was buzz-cut, and she wore faded jeans and flannel.

The couple couldn't have been more opposite, but Brigid saw what Wash did. They were gentle and thoughtful with Didi, but both had steel in their eyes when Jitters filled them in on what was going on at Miller's Range. They'd volunteered to follow Brigid and Carwyn without question.

"This is all a bit mad," Brigid said. "We're going into a paramilitary situation with a team of amateurs to extract twenty-three children we know nothing about."

"We know many of them have been taken from their parents," Carwyn said. "We know they're children and some bastard is planning to sell them to God-knows-who." A dark expression settled over his face. "There are some nights, darling girl, that I question the God I serve. I do not understand why he lets evildoers live."

She turned to him and nudged his face down so she could kiss his cheek. "We don't know the whys, but you and I can be the ones who end them."

He met her eyes. "You are the greatest gift of my eternity."

Brigid couldn't speak. If she did, he would think she was being dramatic.

He was the reason she stayed alive.

———

LATER THAT NIGHT, Brigid sat in the passenger seat of Jitters's reclaimed military transport truck, complete with an army-green tarp tied over the back, as he drove south past Miller's Range.

"There's a turnoff about a mile south of the place," he said. "Then this baby should be able to get over the brush and all that. It's fairly level."

"Level enough that they'll be able to spot this equipment?" There were several crates of TNT in the back of the truck along with barrels and other junk they'd use to hide it.

"Well, I'm guessing that'll depend on how closely they've surveyed that section of the desert," Jitters said. "If they haven't paid too close attention, they're not going to notice a few rusted old barrels that look like they got tossed out the back of a truck fifty years ago. If they've swept it clean, they'll find it."

"Here's hoping they're negligent."

The idea was to set up the improvised explosive devices that night and set them off just after dusk to create a distraction. The combination of the explosions and the people Daniel was trying to drum up from his activist connections in Los Angeles should be enough to keep the company's attention focused at the gate instead of the back dormitories where the children were kept. If the backup was diverted to the front to keep order, Carwyn and Lupe would have an easier time getting the kids out.

Brigid had decided that as much as she wanted to protect the children, the best place for her was in the gate operation, causing as much chaos as possible and keeping an eye on the armed men at the gate. She would have to trust the kids to her husband's enormous heart and simply pray he didn't reveal that he was an earth vampire to anyone who happened across him.

Trusting, trusting man.

"Have you used dynamite before?" Brigid asked.

"I used to work for a mining company," he said. "Along with some other stuff. I know the basics."

And the basics would be all they needed. Dynamite in barrels goes boom. Pesky civilians shouting through megaphones and honking horns. Brigid was confident that for these men, that would be enough to distract them.

Daniel was squeezed in the back, furiously texting on his phone.

"How many people so far?" Brigid asked.

"I have two organizers I'm waiting to hear back from. One was adamant that their group was nonviolent only. I'm a little worried they'll take off when the dynamite goes."

"So tell them ten minutes after the hour," Brigid said. "By the time they show up, it'll just be chaos and shouting, no more boom."

Jitters said, "Well, there will be that last—"

"We don't need to tell Daniel's friends all our plans, Jitters. Let some things be a surprise."

Daniel looked up from his phone. "Wait, what?"

"Nothing," Brigid said. "How many people so far?"

"I think about thirty?"

"That's a good start." Brigid wanted utter and complete chaos. "Keep calling people."

"It's three in the morning."

"It's an emergency. Keep calling."

———

THEY SET the barrels up at quarter-mile intervals zigzagged across the landscape. The idea was to have the explosions timed five minutes apart, slowly coming closer to the front gate to cause the most confusion and hopefully draw the attention of the front guards out of the compound. The last barrel was the riskiest and the one Brigid questioned the most. It would be easily visible from the front gate.

"Maybe this is too close." She could see the lights of the front gate in the distance. "If they have night vision cameras or scopes, they can see us easily."

Jitters and Wash rolled the most rusted barrel from the back of the blacked-out truck.

"If they had night vision scopes, they'd have probably shot at us already," Jitters said. "We can't do anything about it now. If they find 'em, they find 'em. Either way, they're gonna be thinking in this direction and not the other one, especially once Daniel's friends show up."

"If Daniel's friends show up," she muttered.

Wash grinned. "Oh, they will. Nothing a bunch of Los Angeles and Orange County do-gooders love more than a noisy protest in front of a bunch of quasigovernment agents dressed in black. Hell, these assholes won't know what hit them. Daniel knows people who make themselves official nuisances professionally."

"Here's hoping they come through." Brigid watched Wash and Jitters wiring up the detonator and carefully covering it with sand. "Wash, yer goin' to camp out here for the day?"

He nodded toward a low hill covered in grey boulders. "I got a spot out there I've actually camped at before. I'll stay out here, keep an eye on all this stuff, and make sure no one gets curious."

"Good man." Brigid was actually beginning to like these odd desert dwellers even if they did believe in government conspiracies and faked moon landings. They were surprisingly resourceful and didn't seem to mind hard work.

For the front operation, Wash and Daniel would be the primary operatives. And in the back, Carwyn had recruited Oso and Lupe—who really needed to avoid any police—to be his liaisons with the children. Didi, Crystal, and Ronnie would be along to provide support and carry any children who couldn't run.

Brigid would be in front, keeping her eyes out for the unexpected spoiler in the operation. If there was anything she knew about this kind of plan, there was always, always a spoiler.

CHAPTER TWENTY-TWO

Carwyn stood at the mouth of the tunnel with Lupe, Oso, Ronnie, Crystal, and Didi.

"You made this in two nights?" Crystal was examining the walls. "How?"

He debated what to tell her. "It's technology out of Wales actually. Lots of coal mining. Historically speaking."

"Wow."

Didi and Ronnie appeared to be the most nervous. "What time do we go through?"

"We can go through whenever you want, but I don't know how comfortable you are in tunnels." He glanced at Lupe. "Time?"

"It's six thirty-seven."

"We've got at least twenty-three minutes before anything happens."

Didi stared at the tunnel opening. "How far is it?"

"A quarter mile through the tunnel, then a quarter mile across the compound to the dormitories."

Crystal was standing next to Didi. "How you feeling, Miz Dee? You feeling up for this?"

Carwyn was starting to have his doubts. With Ronnie, Crystal, and Oso, they had five adults to help with the little ones. He could carry three children easily.

"Maybe you should stay here with Jitters," Carwyn said. "Keep the truck going and arrange everything in the back there. You could be a welcoming face when we return. The little ones are likely to be a bit scared."

Crystal was nodding silently behind Didi's back. "I think that's a good idea, Miz Dee."

The old woman firmed her jaw. "I told Lupe I'd help. You all think I'm too old now?"

"Hardly," Carwyn said. "But we don't want you to do anything you're nervous..."

Didi stepped forward, flicked on her flashlight, and started walking into the tunnel.

Carwyn watched as her old denim jacket disappeared into the darkness. "Okay then."

Lupe smiled. "I told you. She's tough."

He held out his hand. "After you, my dear."

Lupe looked at her watch again. "Six forty-two."

Carwyn nodded. "We better get walking. We don't want to miss our window."

One by one, they disappeared into the earth, a mismatched troop of rescuers operating on faith and good intentions.

Carwyn looked at the sky and saw the first stars start to peek through scattered clouds. "Are you ready, darling girl?"

———

BRIGID WAS PERCHED in Wash's hideout, watching through binoculars as a crowd of demonstrators started to gather at the gates of Miller's Range. There were signs and a wild collection of mismatched cars, trucks, and vans. Many of the vehicles were painted with slogans like FAMILIES BELONG TOGETHER and END ILLEGAL DETENTION NOW. Others had messages as varied as END THE ALIEN COVER-UP and AREA 51 IS REAL!

"See?" Wash said. "I told you. Danny's friends love shit like this."

"I don't get the alien fascination."

Wash shrugged. "You see some weird shit out here in the desert, Ms. Connor."

"Apparently. So what's your bet? Will they all stay when the boom goes up?" she muttered. "The men at the gate aren't paying much attention to them so far."

"They're moving the kids out tomorrow morning, right? They probably think they can just ride this out."

Brigid pulled her reinforced phone from her pocket. "Seven more minutes."

Car after car lined up along the road that led to Miller's Range. Wash lifted his binoculars. "Holy hell, I think I see a news van."

Brigid couldn't decide if that was good or bad. She definitely didn't want to run into any news people herself, but would that cause the administration of the base to show more restraint or try to make a bigger statement?

"Two minutes," Wash said, watching his phone. "I'm texting Daniel."

"Do it."

Daniel was in the middle of the protesters who'd begun

marching at the gate. Some appeared to be forming a human chain to block the entrance and the exit.

"No, no, no." Brigid tugged on Wash's arm. "Tell Daniel to get them away from the gates. If they block the front gates, the guards may start looking at alternate routes out, which will draw their attention to the back of the range and the area where Carwyn will be taking the children."

"I mean, I'll tell him." Wash had the phone up to his ear. "But I know how these things go sometimes. They kind of take on a life of their own." He waited, then spoke into the phone. "Danny?"

Brigid stared at the growing chaos at the guardhouse. The armed men hadn't originally looked worried, but the fear was growing.

"Yeah, man, you've gotta get them away from the exit. If the front gets blocked, they might start looking back where we gotta get the kids—"

Kaboom!

Wash's voice was drowned out by the first explosion of dynamite. Protesters screamed and some ran toward their cars as others yelled at their compatriots to hold their positions. The explosion got the immediate attention of the contractors. She saw movement past the gate and searchlights trained on the empty field across the road where more IEDs were hidden.

Brigid tapped Wash's arm. "Stay here. Make sure no one comes close to the barrels. I'm going in."

She had to make sure that as the gates were blocked, the attention in the compound stayed in the front. No matter what happened, they could not start looking toward the back of the range. If they did, the entire operation would be blown.

THE FIRST EXPLOSION was their signal to emerge from the tunnel, and Carwyn was ready.

"Follow me." As they exited the tunnel and jogged toward the dormitories at the back of the compound, he saw searchlights begin to sweep across the perimeter. Since they were well inside the fence line, he wasn't worried about being seen, but it did heighten the tension in the group.

"Focus," he said. "They're not going to be paying attention to us if we stay away from the fence."

"How much longer?" Lupe was huffing a little. "Do you see them?"

Carwyn saw the lights in the distance and knew their target was getting nearer. "When we get within sight of it, you hang back. I'll take care of the guards and get their keys."

"What if they don't have keys?" Lupe asked. "What if someone else keeps them?"

"Then I'll knock the doors down," he said. "Trust me—it won't be the first time."

Oso nodded. "I can believe that."

They made their way across the junk-strewn landscape, winding through the carcasses of old Jeeps and broken-down trucks. Carwyn paused at the edge of the junkyard, spotting a Jeep with a bright orange X on the side, which was within clear sight of the block that housed the children. They were deep in the shadows of a truck skeleton, so he crouched behind the Jeep, turned, and faced his small troop.

Didi was puffing but determined. Ronnie and Crystal were a little red in the face but steady. Lupe had the energy of a seventeen-year-old, and Oso was breathing hard. Given a few minutes, he could tell they'd all be fine. Adrenaline was a wondrous drug.

"Here's how it's going to go," he started. "I'll break or open the doors. Then you go in your teams. Ronnie and Oso, Crystal and Didi, Lupe and me. According to Brigid, there were twelve rooms total. That's four rooms for each team. I'm going to break and go. Break and go. We don't have time for anything else."

All of them nodded.

"Get the older kids to help the younger," he continued, "and tell them to hurry. As soon as you have everyone, meet back here." He patted the bright orange X on the Jeep. "This is the meeting spot. We all come back here."

Everyone nodded again.

He motioned for all of them to stay down, then looked across the field between the junkyard and the dormitory.

Brigid's distraction was working. As far as Carwyn could see, there were only two men with rifles patrolling the building, and both of them had their eyes trained toward the front of the compound.

"Stay here," he whispered to Oso. "Wait for my signal."

Carwyn moved swiftly through the darkness, eating up the last few yards of ground that were lit by security lights. He was a silent predator, as most vampires were, and by the time he'd reached the first guard, the man barely had time to turn before Carwyn was on him.

"Who—?"

A swift blow to the head knocked the guard to the ground. Carwyn picked up his rifle, took the ammunition, and twisted the barrel of the weapon into a useless piece of scrap. Then he dragged the unconscious body of the guard toward the dark perimeter and stuffed him behind some bushes.

He paused at the corner of the building, waiting to let his ears take in the surroundings, and heard nothing but the ongoing hubbub at the front gate. He didn't hear guards rushing from the front or vehicles revving their engines.

But dammit, he'd forgotten to listen behind. Carwyn froze seconds before he felt the barrel of a gun tapping his shoulder. He slowly turned.

"Oh." He grinned at the surprisingly large human. "What's that?"

The man's face seemed set in a permanent scowl. "What's what? And who are you?"

Carwyn plastered a confused look on his face. "They didn't tell you I'd be coming by?"

"Who?" The scowl didn't change a bit.

Carwyn put both his fists on his hips and tried to look affronted. "I tell you, it's absolutely rude the way they act like what I do isn't important. I know that cable companies don't have the best reputation for showing up on time, but you'd think—"

"Did you say the cable company?" The scowl turned to confusion.

"Aye, the office got a call that the Wi-Fi was out, and I was in the area doing some repairs, so" —as the barrel of the guard's rifle drooped, Carwyn grabbed it, yanked it from the man's hands, and flipped it to bash the guard's forehead— "I thought I'd drop by."

The man's eyes crossed and bright red blood bloomed between his eyebrows. He blinked rapidly before he tumbled to the ground.

Carwyn twisted the rifle into a useless piece of metal and tossed it into the darkness. Then he dragged the second guard toward the dark perimeter, hoping that rifle butt had done its job. He reached down and felt around the man's waist, but just like with the first guard, he couldn't feel any keys.

"Damn." He heard a second explosion go off in the distance, put his fingers to his lips, and let out a short, sharp whistle.

Oso, Lupe, and the rest of the gang ran from the darkness and toward the dorms.

"No keys," Carwyn whispered. "Guards are out and their guns are useless. I'm going to start breaking doors."

Everyone nodded and followed Carwyn to the first door on the bottom floor. Once he got there, he knew why there were no keys. "Combination keypads."

Oso looked at them but shook his head. "I have an electronic key for those things, but I didn't bring it."

"Here's where sheer size is a bonus." Carwyn put his shoulder to the door, backed up, and tried to make it look difficult when he broke the door down. "Lupe?"

The girl shoved past the broken pieces of door and entered the room. "Hola?"

Two elementary-school-aged children were huddled in the back corner.

Lupe crouched down and held out her arms. "Come with us," she said in Spanish. "We're going to get you out and find your parents."

The older boy's eyes darted from Carwyn's massive frame to Lupe's open arms.

"Come on," Lupe said. "I promise he's a friend."

Carwyn smiled and held out his hand. The little girl huddled with the boy jumped up and merrily ran to Carwyn.

"Kika!" the boy yelled.

"Come." Oso stepped through the door and spoke to the boy. "We don't have time. Do you want the soldiers to find us?"

The boy, seemingly convinced, ran to his bed and grabbed a pillowcase from under it, then ran to the door where Oso and Ronnie were standing.

"One down." Carwyn hoisted the little girl into one arm. "Eleven to go."

———

THE THIRD CHARGE went off just as Brigid made her way through the crowd and up to the gate. The shouting mass of protesters had only grown since the first explosion occurred. There were two news vans now, and another vehicle with glaring lights seemed to be making its way down the crowded road that led to Miller's Range.

Brigid heard sirens in the distance and wondered who had called the sheriff's office. It had to be one of the protesters or one of the media.

She had been banking on an opening somewhere along the gate, but so far she'd been disappointed. She wanted in. She needed in. The protest was growing and, as Wash had predicted, was taking on a life of its own. She needed to be able to read the mood of the men inside the gates.

She'd deliberately dressed in clothes similar to the contractors' with a black bulletproof vest and an added neck guard she hoped no one noticed. As she crept along the gate and back into the shadows, she noticed all the personnel at the gate were focused on the protesters and the media. Many were speaking into radios, and most were looking frantically over their shoulders, clearly expecting backup.

Excellent. They had them exactly where they wanted them.

The fourth explosion rocked the air, even closer than the previous three. Screams went up from the crowd of protesters, guards shouted, and in the chaos, Brigid scrambled up and over the fence, vaulting herself over the coil of concertina wire at the top and landing softly inside the gates at Miller's Range.

She was in.

CHAPTER TWENTY-THREE

B y the sixth dorm room, Carwyn was fairly certain they had most of the smallest children. There were two so small that they had to be carried by Lupe and Ronnie. Both were whimpering, though it hadn't turned into an all-out cryfest.

Yet.

He kept going with the doors. Seventh door was Ronnie and Oso. He saw two teen girls staring at them with wide eyes.

Eighth door belonged to Didi and Crystal. A teenage girl and a preteen boy followed them eagerly.

Ninth door was his and Lupe's. He busted down the door to see two teen girls, both of whom were crouched in defensive positions. One held a makeshift knife made from a piece of scrap metal, and the other had ripped a lamp from the wall and was brandishing it.

"We're friends." Carwyn shifted the little girl in his arms and held up a hand. "We're here to get you out."

Lupe held out her free hand. "Come with us," she said in Spanish. "The men holding you are going to sell you."

"We know," the girl with the knife replied in English. "How do we know you're not the same?"

Lupe looked with wide eyes between Carwyn and the baby in her arms. "We're not. I mean... Why would we—?"

"Fine." The girl with the knife wrapped it in a scrap of cloth and stuffed it in a pocket. "If you're the same, at least you're stupider." She barked something at the other girl in Spanish. "Come on."

The two girls followed Carwyn and Lupe out of the building. The girl with the knife walked ahead and guided them. "There's no one in this room. The girl was crying constantly and then nothing. I think they got rid of her."

Carwyn and Lupe exchanged a worried look.

"When?" Lupe asked.

"A couple of weeks ago."

Lupe nodded and looked at Carwyn. "It might have been the girl in LA," she whispered. "She said she ran away when they were moving her. That's all I know."

"I need to open it," Carwyn said. "To be sure."

The girl who'd held the knife shrugged but took the little girl who'd been in Carwyn's arms. He broke down the door and saw what looked like the remains of an occupied room, but no one was inside.

"Told you," the girl said. "They probably killed her. She was stupid. The next door has two boys. They're like ten or something."

Carwyn took out that door too and then motioned for Ronnie and Oso to go inside. The tough girl continued with her guided tour. She was more than a little talkative, but something about it told Carwyn she was working off nervous energy. There was a bite to her voice, though that was more than understandable considering the circumstances.

"Are you guys the ones making all the noise at the front? I was wondering what was going on." She led them around the corner to the last two rooms on the south side of the dorms. "Two more girls like us here, then one in the next room unless she's gone too."

"Your English is really good," Lupe said. "Did you learn in school?"

"I mean, I guess so, but I'm from El Centro, so I kind of grew up speaking English." She shot Lupe a derisive look. "You think they only take migrants here? They take anyone. I made a mistake and trusted the wrong person. That's the only reason I'm here."

"We'll get you home," Carwyn said. "We have people working—"

"I'm not going home," the girl said. "Forget that." She pointed at the door. "Here."

Carwyn broke down the door and motioned for Crystal and Didi to go inside. "One more?"

"Yeah, just the one. Then where are we gonna—?"

"STOP!"

Carwyn froze, trying to determine where the voice was coming from. He'd been so distracted by the girl he'd failed to see the man in the black BDUs come from the shadows in the direction of the mess hall.

He was pointing a gun at them. "Stop where you are." The man fumbled for the radio on his shoulder.

Carwyn looked at Lupe, who was already moving behind him with the baby in her arms.

Good girl.

"You!"

Carwyn saw the girl who'd been leading them strike from the corner of his eye. The child she'd been holding was gone, but the knife was back. She rushed at the guard, plunging the weapon into the man's belly and yanking the radio from his hand.

———

BRIGID WALKED CASUALLY ALONG the edge of the shadows, trying to mimic the stance of the soldiers in the compound. She hadn't seen any women so far, but her short hair and confident walk seemed to skate under the radar of the men she passed, who were all focused on the growing commotion at the gate. The media vans were filming, and most of the squawk on the radios and the muffled arguments she heard seemed to be focused on them.

"—get them away from the gate. If they see any identifying—"

"Are we supposed to open the gates? I thought O'Neill said someone in the sheriff's office—"

"—fucking sheriff's office is useless. Try our contact at border—"

"Local police going to be a problem?"

"—four trucks showing up in the morning to deal with the cargo, and we can't have—"

"—we're going to have to look at other options."

"O'Neill's not going to like that."

"Too bad."

Their goal had been to cause a distraction to allow the

kids to escape, and they appeared to have accomplished that. Now, however, their distraction had become a liability. There were only two roads out of the compound, the one in good repair at the front gate and the broken one that cut directly across the path Carwyn and the children would have to take to reach the tunnel opening.

Cargo.

What were they referring to? Was it the people only or was there something else these mercenaries were trading? Brigid found it hard to believe they'd need four trucks to deal with twenty-some children and teens, so she had a suspicion that something else was going on. Drugs? Weapons? It could be anything.

Brigid kept to the dark edge of the walkway and kept her head down as she marched deeper into the heart of the compound. Since her first survey, she'd noted the large warehouse where the SUVs were parked outside in a neat line. It was in front of both the mess hall and the dormitories, directly behind the main clerical office and a decent distance from the gates. It was the heart of the compound, now that she thought about it. The most security surrounding it. The most personnel. Whatever they were guarding, it was going to be there. The kids had always been secondary.

"Hey!"

Brigid knew someone had spotted her. She kept walking.

"Hey you!"

She pretended not to know they were talking to her. She walked faster but didn't run until she got to the line of dark SUVs behind the office. Once she spotted a viable shadow, she ducked into it, sped away at vampire speed, and left her follower behind.

"What the hell?"

"Who was that?"

She could hear them from her perch in a cottonwood tree between the front office and the old garage.

"There's someone in here who doesn't belong." A radio squawked. "104, we have an intruder spotted behind main office, over."

The man with her follower asked, "How do you know it's an intruder? Maybe they just—"

"It was a woman." He picked up his radio again. "104, do you read, over?"

"Affirmative, Carson. Where are you—?"

"There's an intruder, 104, numbers only." The man kept his voice low, but Brigid could hear it all. "I'm currently between Position B and Position D. Please advise."

"Are you alone, 205?"

"213 is with me."

"Stay together, search for the intruder, detain, and report in ten."

"You'll spread the word?"

"I'm on it. Description?"

"Slim female, five six or seven. Athletic build. Skinny even. Short dark hair. Vest and neck guard."

"On it. I'll alert the gate guard."

"Why alert the...?" The man called 205 huffed out a breath and hung his radio on his shoulder. "Why alert the guardhouse?" He muttered, "It's not like they're going to admit they have a breach."

"Maybe she's on the payroll?" the man named 213 said. "Maybe we just haven't met her yet?"

"You think O'Neill's going to hire a female? In this place?"

The other man laughed darkly. "Good point."

"Come on." The two men headed in the direction of the warehouse. "Let's make sure everything is secure."

What was *everything*? Brigid lowered herself from the easy perch in the tree and made her way to the side of the warehouse where she could see a rusted staircase leading to the second floor.

What are you hiding, boys?

She climbed the staircase, cringing with every squeak and creak. After what seemed like an eternity, she reached the door, only to find it locked.

Damn. Where was her brute of a husband when she needed him?

———

THE GIRL HOLDING the knife grabbed the radio on the guard's shoulder and tossed it on the ground. She stomped on it, then pulled the knife out of the man, swung her arm back farther, and stabbed him again, going deeper and higher on the second strike, directly under his bulletproof vest and into his soft, unprotected side.

"You fucker!" she growled. "You think you can touch me and live? I told you I'd kill you, mother*fucker*."

Carwyn was frozen as the girl executed the man with little more than a filed piece of scrap metal. The guard had stood no chance against her speed, fury, and excellent aim.

As he slumped to the ground, a trickle of blood came from the corner of the man's mouth. The girl with the knife pulled it out of the guard's belly and spat on his face as he collapsed.

The girl turned to the rest of them and didn't even flinch. "He raped me and my roommate." She pointed to the quiet girl holding a baby. "I told him I'd kill him, and he beat me up." She looked over her shoulder. "You laughing now, you motherfucker?"

"Language, Celia." The girl's roommate was barely audible. "There are little kids here."

"Whatever." The girl looked around. "Hey, big man, why don't you break the last door so we can get the hell out of here, okay?"

Ignoring the girl's imperious tone, Carwyn walked to the last door and pushed it in with one shoulder, shoving the broken barrier aside for Ronnie and Crystal to grab the teen girl he saw cowering in a corner. Carwyn pointed at Oso and snapped his fingers, pointing toward the dark junkyard. Oso nodded; then he, Lupe, and Didi started moving the rest of the kids to the end of the dorms and toward the darkness.

Carwyn walked over to the girl called Celia, who was standing over the man she'd stabbed, watching him slowly bleed out. The guard's eyes were wide and staring. Blood dripped from his lips and he moved his mouth as if to speak, but no sound came out.

"Is there anyone else?" he asked.

Celia looked at the other rooms. "No. I was counting the kids just before I saw this motherfucker. Those last two make twenty-three."

"What happened to the other two?"

"One of the babies is gone. I don't know what they did with him—he was really young, probably not even a year. One of the guards might have taken him or something. The other one was the crying girl, and you already checked her room. She's gone."

Carwyn didn't want to take a chance. He jogged down the rest of the dormitory, but he didn't smell any humans in the rooms, so he walked back to Celia. He bent down and picked up the dying guard's gun. He bent it in half while Celia watched. Then he bent down and snapped the man's neck.

"A wound like that," he said grimly, "is a slow and painful death."

Celia nodded. "I know."

Carwyn met her dark eyes, held her stare, and the girl didn't flinch, not even at the giant standing in front of her. "Come on," he said. "The little ones need us to get to get them out."

"I'd never hurt any of the kids."

"I know." Carwyn looked down at the dead man. "If I doubted that, you wouldn't be coming with us."

CHAPTER TWENTY-FOUR

Giovanni had told her it was possible, but she'd never really tried. Brigid held the flame in her hand and tried to concentrate it, gripping the metal doorknob and focusing the heat her body produced into the lock that kept her from finding out what was in the warehouse. She could hear voices inside and hoped that the cover of night was enough to conceal her from the men below who were looking for her.

She felt the metal heat; then it slowly started to smell. It began to glow softly, eventually turning from a cherry red to a dusty white. She pushed it, and the metal collapsed like wet cardboard.

"Well fuck me sideways," she muttered. "Can't believe that worked." Watch her lockpick anything from now on! Doors meant nothing to her. "Now, let's see what you naughty boys are up to."

Brigid pulled the creaking door out with the edge of a baton she had tucked into her waistband. The metal was already weakened; unfortunately, that didn't make the hinges any less squeaky.

"What was that?"

She darted into the nearest shadow and pressed herself against the wall when the siren chirped.

"Probably just a rat." There were two more men, both wearing the same black BDUs and vests that the men outside wore. On the back of their vest, CANYON SECURITY was emblazoned in white block letters.

The man angled his neck to his radio. "Carson, you seeing anything outside?"

"Did you see something? Fuck me, I told you, Jason!"

"Hey, I thought we were only doing numbers."

The men in the warehouse were confused. "What the hell are you two arguing about?"

"We saw a woman outside, heading toward the warehouse, over."

"Did'ja call O'Neill?"

"Numbers, 301! Fucking use your numbers, for fuck's sake."

"Whatever." He snapped off his radio. "God, this guy's such a douche. I wish O'Neill'd never moved these guys in."

"We need the extra manpower with all the extra cargo though."

"Do we?" The man walked over and lifted an edge of the crate. "I mean, a couple of forklifts, a few trucks, and we're in the money." He shook his head. "No more pissant requisition forms, right?"

The second guard lifted what looked like a brick of white powder from the crate. "How much for just this one?"

"I got no fucking idea, but O'Neill knows. That's all I care about."

So they were moving drugs. Sounded like they might have been legitimate government contractors at one point, but they were way past that. These mercenaries hadn't just put coyotes out of business, they'd *become* the coyotes.

"Did you hear that?"

Brigid froze, but it wasn't her making the noise.

No, it was the steps leading up to her second-floor perch that were creaking, and creaking fast.

She moved farther down the walkway, trying to move as carefully as possible so as not to alert the men on the floor of the warehouse.

"213, what happened to the door?"

"Looks like someone brought a torch," the guard said. "It's completely compromised."

"I'm calling backup."

The voices were getting closer. Brigid crept to the highest stack of boxes she could find, swung herself over, and dropped to the top of the crates as quietly as possible.

"What was that?"

"I'm telling you, I'd a—"

"If you say a fucking rat again, I'm gonna punch your dick. That wasn't a fucking rat." A beam of light swung wildly around the warehouse. "Screw this—I'm turning the main lights on."

With only seconds to spare, Brigid swung down from the top of a loaded pallet to the ground. She landed softly and pressed her nose to the cardboard next to her.

Jesus wept, that wasn't cocaine as she'd thought. This was one hundred percent pure, medical-grade heroin.

Brigid's mouth watered and her fangs dropped on instinct. The urge to bury her face in the sweet smell was nearly overwhelming, but she fought it back. It was exactly as she'd told Daniel; the hunger was screaming at her, but she knew it would never be sated. It never could be. Even a human high on heroin wasn't a good substitute.

The guards were talking into their radios as Brigid nearly blissed out on the scent of the drug she'd always crave. The memories of oblivion smashed into her brain, reminding her of every euphoric high that had taken her away from reality.

Snap out of it.

Brigid slapped her cheek and bit viciously into her forearm to shake the fuzziness from her brain. Funnily enough, her mind never reminded her about the puking or the body aches or the fevers. She never remembered any of the bad stuff, just the sweet purple oblivion of the drugs.

"Did you hear that?" The torch beam swung dangerously close to the crate where she was hiding. "I'm calling O'Neill."

Brigid sat on the ground, her back against the pallet of heroin, silently debating what she should do.

"I don't fucking have time to deal with this shit." A snarling voice, heavy with smoker's growl, entered the warehouse. "I got these fucking hippies at the front gates, two dead guards, and an empty dormitory, so *what the hell do you want from me, McGill?*"

"Captain, there's someone in the warehouse."

"So find them, you useless ball sack, and kill them while I go track down those fucking girls! I've got buyers to meet in the morning, and this isn't part of the plan."

Empty dorms? Tracking down girls? Well, they didn't need to be doing that. It looked like fate had decided for her.

The foolish men of Canyon Security Company needed another distraction to keep their attention focused away from Carwyn's kids.

Brigid flicked a lighter and gathered a ball of fire in her hand before she lobbed it up and over the pallet, where it landed smack in the middle of the arguing men.

"What the hell is that?" someone screamed.

"Molotov cocktail!" another yelled. "The hippies are in the building. They got in!"

Brigid laughed and lobbed another one.

This was going to be fun.

———

IN THE DISTANCE, an alarm went up. Carwyn and Oso exchanged a final look as the man ducked his head into the tunnel and followed the kids who'd already entered the darkness.

"Go," Carwyn said. "Don't wait for me. Get the children back to Liberty Springs. I'm going to make sure Brigid is okay and that no one is following you."

Oso's eyes went wide. "Man, what are you doing?"

"I'll be fine. Don't worry about it. And I'll take care of this tunnel. Trust me, it'll look like nothing was ever here. Just get in the truck and drive away. Jitters will take care of you all until Brigid and I get there."

"Lupe's gonna freak."

Carwyn put a hand on the man's shoulder. "Then it looks like you're going to have to reassure them. All of them. I'll be back soon, Oso. Just hang in there and get back to the Springs."

He turned without another thought. It wasn't that he doubted Brigid. Far from it. He just wanted to make sure she didn't do anything she'd regret later.

———

BRIGID WALKED THROUGH the burning warehouse, lighting things on fire as the sprinkler system put them out. It wasn't a great system. Newer systems *poured* water onto flames. This was more of a gentle shower, far from enough to quench the kind of flames she was throwing out.

"There!"

A punch in the chest told her that another bullet had hit her armor. She could recover from nearly anything that didn't destroy her head or pierce her spine, but she didn't want to chance the gun-happy guards in this place. She slipped between two burning pallets and felt the heat dancing along her skin.

"Are you just playing, ye thick bollocks?" She tossed another ball of flame near the door to keep them from escaping. "Throw something useful at me, ye tools."

There was indistinct shouting all around her. Brigid felt the flames inside herself, aching to get out, aching to snap and consume. She could eat the evil men who peddled drugs and traded in children. What would happen to them otherwise? Should she trust a human government to punish them?

No.

"The warehouse! Everything's burning!"

"Get the pallets out!" a gritty voice screamed at the men. "Get the forklift. Get them out!"

She flexed her shoulders and removed the bulletproof

vest. She unhooked the neck guard and walked to the center of the warehouse, ash and water creating black rivulets running down her bare skin.

Brigid looked for the man they called O'Neill. He was an old, wrinkled wreck of a man with a sneering mouth and a buzz-cut head. His eyes locked on her, and she saw his eyes grow wide in confusion as he mouthed, *What the fuck?*

She pointed at him and smiled. Then Brigid held out her arms, released the fire, and flames rolled out from her body as the hungry inferno consumed everything.

———

CARWYN FOUND her sitting naked on a rise overlooking the burning warehouse. She'd found a tarp to drape around her shoulders, and a solid inch of her velvet-brown hair was burned at the nape.

He sat next to her and watched the fire. "Good distraction. I'd say it might be overkill, but one of the kidnapped girls stabbed a guard with a piece of old license plate, so I probably don't have any moral high ground to preach from."

"They were shipping drugs." Her eyes were locked on the burn. "Heroin. Very high grade."

Always a sore subject. He ran a gentle hand over her hair. "They won't be shipping it now."

"The warehouse collapsed with men in it. Probably a dozen or so. Maybe more."

"I killed the guard the girl stabbed. He might have survived if someone found him, but we didn't have time and I made a split-second decision."

"It wasn't split-second for me," Brigid said. "I wanted all of them to die."

"Why?"

"They stole kids. Talked about them like they were just another thing to trade. Drugs. Weapons. Children. And they'd probably get away with it. The children will remember this trauma their whole lives. Every single day, they'll remember the fear."

She would know. He put his arm around her waist and pulled her head to his shoulder.

She remembered. Every night.

"Are you looking for absolution, Saint Brigid?"

"Maybe."

"I can't offer you any, for I don't think you did a wrong." And maybe that was wrong of him, but that was also the world they lived in.

She looked up, and her eyes were still the most beautiful sight of his eternity, whiskey gold burned grey around the iris. Immortal eyes. Eyes that saw pain and chose kindness.

"Justice," Carwyn whispered, "doesn't always mend with mercy. Sometimes it mends with blood."

"Are the children safe?" She shook her head. "As if you'd be here if they weren't."

"I'll always run after you, sweet girl." He kissed the top of her head. "I'm a fool in love with my darling."

Fire engines were turning in to the compound, breaking through the gates, with protesters following in their wake.

"They'll find evidence of the children in the dormitories," Carwyn said. "But you need to come with me now, my Brigid; we don't want them to find the tunnel."

"Right." She rose and threw off the tarp. "Nothing like a

naked run in the desert to finish off a night of fire and destruction."

"That's the spirit." He stripped off his pants and left them in the dirt.

"My God." Brigid covered her eyes. "The full moon isn't so bright as that arse."

Carwyn tossed his shirt in the air with a giant *whoop* and ran, naked as the day he was born, as the woman he adored beyond reason followed him, her rueful laugh lifting his heart higher than the stars.

CHAPTER TWENTY-FIVE

B rigid stood by the fire in Didi's compound as the misfit residents of Liberty Springs came together in the middle of the night to set up tents, sleeping bags, warm blankets, pillows, air mattresses, and anything else they could find to make the frightened refugees from Miller's Range comfortable and welcome.

The children were still in shock, but Brigid could already see the astonishing resilience of youth emerging through the traumatic night. Siblings who had been separated were together again. Babies were being held by experienced and loving arms.

Lupe, Ronnie, and Crystal were making a game of guessing names and ages with the children, trying to garner bits of information that might help them find their families. Stuffed animals and a few dolls had magically appeared, only to be clutched in nervous arms as twenty-three children and teens tried to make sense of yet another new reality.

Didi had put the older girls to work making chili and hot

chocolate for the younger children, knowing wisely that activity and direction were often the best medicine.

Wash, Oso, Daniel, and their group of friends were organizing tents and watch teams for the rest of the night, determined to stand guard over the group until Daniel's friend from an immigrant-rights group and Lupe's lawyer came in the morning.

Carwyn walked up to Brigid and stuck his large hands in the back pockets of her jeans. "So I just made a call that's liable to give Giovanni and Beatrice headaches."

"Did you warn them?"

"I did. After I made the call."

"To?"

"Ernesto's people."

"Oh lovely." Brigid closed her eyes and shook her head. "Beatrice will have your hide the next time she sees you. She told you not to get her grandfather involved."

"That's why it's better to ask forgiveness than permission," he said. "Let's face it—technically, this is all Ernesto's territory."

"And none of this had a whiff of vampire interference before we came along and got involved." That was the rule in Los Angeles, and it was the same in Dublin. Unless a vampire was involved in the crime, human authorities were in charge. Patrick didn't involve himself in solely human matters, and neither did Ernesto. "What were you thinking?"

Carwyn nodded at the little children sitting around a fire and drinking mugs of hot chocolate and eating bowls of chili.

"I was thinking of them," he said. "I was thinking that the human government might take months—years even—to find their parents. I was thinking of children lost in a system that doesn't care enough. And I was thinking of all the resources that Ernesto and his people have." He rested his chin on the top of Brigid's head. "You know I did the right thing."

Brigid sighed. "You did the right thing." It would be a mess, but Carwyn was right. Ernesto's people could find these children's parents in days, not weeks or months. And it wasn't until they were safe at home with family who loved them that healing could begin. "We can't save everyone," she said. "You know that, don't you?"

"We saved them." He kissed her temple. "We can't save everyone, but we saved them."

"We did."

"Doesn't that feel good?" He stood behind her and settled his arms around her shoulders, surrounding her in his warm energy.

Brigid stilled in the comfort of her mate's arms, and it was as if the moonlit mountains had embraced her. Everything that was uneven or sideways in her soul shifted and settled with a sigh.

"Why do you want to leave Dublin?" Brigid asked.

"It's a big world out there, darling girl. Don't you want to see a bit more of it?"

"Where would we go?"

"Anywhere you want."

She looked over her shoulder. "And what would we do? I'm not a tourist, Carwyn. I need..." She thought of Daniel Siva's regimented life. His busy calendar that left little time for idleness or too much drifting thought. She thought about her own drive to be working always, to be busy, to be occupied. She turned her head back to the fire.

In many ways, she was just like Daniel, stuck in her own

routine because it was safe, it was predictable, and it kept her from thinking of hungers that couldn't be sated.

"I need things to do," she said. "I need to have a mission."

"I know that." He kissed her head again. "Don't you think I know my wife?"

"So what—?"

"This." He pointed his chin at the campfire. "We'll do this."

"Rescue children from human traffickers?"

"Sometimes. Sometimes we might find a runaway like Lupe. Sometimes we might track down a person who did something wrong."

"Kind of... bounty hunters? Of a sort."

"We'll help people," Carwyn said. "In our own ways, we're both very good at that, don't you think?"

"And we keep the house in Dublin?"

"Why not? Dublin's home, isn't it?"

"Yes." It was home. For now. She was still relatively young in vampire years, and the thought of leaving her aunt, her last human connection in the world, wasn't something she wanted to face. Still, her aunt was in excellent health. She wasn't an old woman. She didn't need Brigid around all the time. "Okay."

"Okay?"

She could hear the smile in his voice. Brigid turned in his arms and looked up. "I'll call Murphy tomorrow night."

A wicked smirk touched the corner of his mouth. "Can you video chat with him? And can I watch? I don't have to be on the call, just... observe from the corner of the room."

"Like a creepy professional voyeur?"

"Yes. Exactly like that."

She shook her head and turned back to the children, who were starting to blink longer and longer as the safety of their surroundings and the warm food began to settle in.

"Yer a strange man, Carwyn ap Bryn."

"You'd be bored if I wasn't."

"Probably."

Definitely.

———

CARWYN AND BRIGID retreated for the day and woke at dusk to a report from Daniel about the goings-on of the day. He and Wash had driven down to Miller's Range and watched the fire department going in and out of the compound. In addition to the local fire department, there were multiple local, state, and federal agencies spotted.

The sheriff was the most prominent until the FBI arrived with a caravan of SUVs and several large trucks. The local news was reporting that a Mexican cartel had been occupying the old army base.

"There was no mention of the contractor." Daniel was sitting on a rock near the mouth of the cave where Carwyn and Brigid were sleeping during the day. The moon was rising and silhouetted a stand of Joshua trees along the ridge.

"So the chances of anyone coming after the children is small," Carwyn said. "That's a relief."

"There wasn't any mention of missing kids on the news," Daniel said. "I mean, they left stuff in their rooms, right?"

"Most of them did," Carwyn said. "They may be keeping those details from the media for the investigation."

"Or because there's a border agent involved," Daniel said.

"Yes, also because of that." Carwyn stretched out his legs. "Either way, I don't think anyone could track the children here. I collapsed the tunnel, and we made sure none of the tracks from the truck were visible. There's no way they would trace them to the Springs unless someone here talked."

Daniel laughed. "No one in the Springs is gonna talk to the cops. You can be sure of that."

"Did the attorney come?" Brigid asked. "Lupe's attorney?"

"Yeah. She and Anna Marie came around lunchtime. Anna Marie talked to all the kids. The lawyer lady talked to Lupe and some of the older girls. Didi and Crystal too. They seemed okay with the kids staying at the Springs for a couple of days. Just said to make sure we watched out so none of them sneaked off, you know?"

"Yes. Especially the older kids." Carwyn had told Brigid about Celia, the girl from El Centro who killed the guard. "How much information did they get from the children?"

"I think most of them had something. Some of them knew their parents' names. One little girl just kept repeating her aunt's phone number, but she didn't know her name, you know? Just Tía. But there was the phone number. The biggest problem is the baby boy. No one seems to know his name or who his mother is."

"And the boy who went missing," Carwyn said. "Do any of the older girls have any idea—?"

"No." Daniel's face grew dark. "I mean, I guess the best guess would be to interview the guards, right? The ones left at the range. They might know what happened to the baby."

Brigid rubbed a hand over her face. "What a nightmare."

"At least it's a nightmare that twenty-three kids avoided," Daniel said.

"I'm praying that someone took the child home," Carwyn said. "Or grew a conscience and returned him to his mother if he was that young. It's possible."

"We need to find the border patrol agent they bribed," Brigid said. "That might be something for Ernesto's people."

"That might give us way more information about all the kids," Daniel said. "Between what Celia can tell us and what that border—"

"Celia?" Carwyn asked. "Why would Celia know— Oh, I'm a knob." He shook his head. "Of course she would know. It all makes sense now."

"What?" Brigid was lost. "Isn't Celia the girl who killed the guard?"

"Yes, and she didn't hesitate for a second." Carwyn looked at Daniel. "She's a coyote, isn't she?"

Daniel shrugged a little. "I mean, I don't think she organized it, but she was the one in charge of the group, you know?"

"The girl?" Brigid was gobsmacked. "That little girl was the smuggler?"

"She was the driver," Daniel said. "She's a citizen, can move freely back and forth across the border. According to her, she was driving a camper van, trying to cross with a bunch of surfboards on the back of the van. She's a regular, so she doesn't usually get stopped. She had one of the older girls in the front, acting like it was a girls' trip to Ensenada, you know?"

"She's a regular," Brigid said. "So the wrong kind of guard gets wind of her cargo and she's a prime target."

"She had twenty people in the back of that camper," Daniel said. "A dozen of them were kids or teenagers trying to get north. The adults got arrested, and she and the kids all got taken to Miller's Range."

"Damn." Brigid rubbed her chin. "Fuck me, I never would have guessed a girl that young—"

"She's not looking to go home," Daniel said. "Said she won't go. She's already talking to Didi about working at her place."

Brigid and Carwyn exchanged a look.

"She's made it this far on her own," Carwyn said. "I have a feeling our advice would go in one ear and out the other."

"I can't disagree." Brigid shrugged. "There are worse places to be than working with Didi. She needs help though. From what she said—"

"She won't get help until she's ready," Carwyn said. "It has to be in her own time. We can keep in touch. Let her decide when she's ready."

"Anna Marie was already talking about getting a trauma counselor out here tomorrow," Daniel said. "She's a really good person. She cares. For real."

"Thank you, Daniel." Brigid smiled at the young man. "You've gone above and beyond on this. You should be proud of yourself."

He looked uncomfortable. "It was the least I could do. After taking Lupe from home... I just hope she'll forgive me. Eventually."

"In time." Brigid patted his hand. "She's young, Daniel. Give it time."

———

LATER, as the children settled in for their second night in Liberty Springs, a shiny black Lincoln drove down the road, kicking up a long trail of dust as it slowly approached the encampment. The smaller children poked their head out of Didi's compound as the older children shoved them back, uncertain in the face of a car that exuded wealth and power.

When the car came to a stop, a uniformed human driver opened the passenger door and Paula de la Cruz, oldest daughter and lieutenant of Don Ernesto Alvarez of Los Angeles, stepped out of the car. She was a light-skinned woman with deep brown hair that fell straight to her waist in a mahogany waterfall. Paula was dressed casually—for Paula—in a pristine white pantsuit and matching coat. Her boots were made of rich brown leather, and she carried an alligator-skin briefcase.

Carwyn stepped forward to greet her. "Paula, it is so lovely to see you again."

She raised an arched eyebrow. "I wish my father was as pleased as you are."

"I don't want to bring up the number of favors that I have done for Don Ernesto, but should I be forced to recall them—"

"You do not need to inform me." She lifted a manicured hand. "I have reminded him of this myself." She looked around the motley group in Didi's compound. "What have you gotten yourself into, Carwyn? Because I don't know you and your wife that well, but I do know this was not Brigid's doing."

Brigid barked out a laugh and covered her mouth. "Paula, do you like hot chocolate? I feel like this is going to take a while to explain."

———

IT WAS near midnight when Carwyn, Brigid, and Lupe pulled up to a brightly lit house in Huntington Park. The white picket fence was securely latched, but Carwyn knew the door was open and Lupe's mother was waiting.

"Are you sure you don't want us to go in with you?" Brigid asked.

"We can tell your mother everything you did," Carwyn said. "Lupe, you're a hero to those children. You're the only one who never gave up on them."

The girl took a deep breath and reached for her backpack. She was dusty and her hair needed a wash. Her clothes were dirty and her shoes were probably destined for the rubbish bin, but her face was determined. Her eyes were confident. She was the same steel-willed girl they'd met days before. Only now she had an air of confidence and assurance. She'd been through the fire and survived.

"I'm okay," Lupe said. "Maybe tomorrow night. For tonight I just want to hug my mom and let her know I'm okay." She smiled. "And take a really long shower and sleep in my own bed."

Brigid nodded. "Good. We'll plan to come over tomorrow night then."

"Okay, cool." She opened the door of the Bronco and paused. "So like... an immigration lawyer. That's something that can really help a lot of people, isn't it?"

"Yes," Carwyn said. "I believe it is."

Lupe nodded. "Yeah. I thought so." She hopped out of the car and walked through the gate just as her mother opened the door. María ran down the steps and embraced Lupe before she could reach the front step.

Carwyn blinked hard.

"Are you crying?" Brigid asked.

"Just a little."

"We'll be paying for her university fees, won't we?"

He sniffed. "Every single one."

"And making sure her legal status is settled?"

"It's the least we can do, Brigid."

"Just making sure." She reached across for his hand and squeezed. "Like you said, it's the least we can do."

EPILOGUE

Patrick Murphy was glaring at the video screen, every polished inch of the man exuding irritation. "Is he forcing you to do this?"

"Forcing me?" Brigid raised her eyebrows. "Tell me yer jokin' with that question, Murphy."

"Fine." He pursed his lips. "Persuading you very forcefully."

"And in what universe have you or that man ever convinced me to do anything I don't want to do?"

He was grumpy. Murphy was grumpy and more than a little pissed off.

"Is Anne there?" Brigid asked.

"No, she's in Belfast visiting her sister."

That explained it. Murphy was like a grumpy little boy without his favorite toy when his mate was away. "No wonder yer in a mood."

"I'm losing my chief of security! Did you think I'd be happy about it?"

"What's Tom then? Chopped liver? I'm telling him you

said that." Brigid was just poking fun at Murphy now. "We're keeping the house, man. We'll still be based there. Do you think I'd not come in a heartbeat if anyone back home needed me?"

He looked slightly mollified. "What the hell are you going to do with your time then?"

"I don't know. Travel a bit. Go to Alaska in the winter and stay out all day. Learn glassblowing and practice my knitting on Carwyn's chest hair. I don't know. I'll do vampire shite and act cool."

Murphy had been with her every step of the way. He was the first person to give her a job after she'd started recovery, and he'd continued to employ her when she was a volatile newborn fire vampire. He knew her as well as a brother.

"You need more than that, Brig. You know you do."

"We're going to be helping people," she said. "We're going to travel and be knights errant or something like that."

"Now that is definitely Carwyn's idea." Murphy rolled his eyes.

"Yes, but it's a good one." She smiled. "You know it is."

Murphy gave her a rueful smile. "Don't let yourself get bored. You light things on fire when you get bored."

"As if Carwyn doesn't know that firsthand," she said. "Come now, you know I'll be busy keeping him out of trouble."

"Where are you headed next?"

Brigid shrugged. "I don't know. Not Europe. Maybe we'll stay in America a little bit longer. Head back to New York. Surf the volcanos in Hawaii. Visit the cowboys in Texas."

Murphy made a face. "You have a strange idea of fun."

"It's an odd place, this country. I could stand to see a little more of it if I'm being honest."

"Don't be gone too long," Murphy said. "You know we're all going to miss you."

"Carwyn and I will be sure to come back by Christmas. Fair?"

"Oh no." Murphy rubbed his forehead. "We don't need the Welshman. Just you will be fine."

Carwyn winked at her from the door. "It's okay, Murphy. I know you hate me for stealing her."

Murphy narrowed his eyes. "Has he been listening this whole time?"

"Not the whole time."

Carwyn had missed the first twenty seconds or so of the call because he'd been trying to convince Zain that he needed to sell them the Bronco.

"Tell the idiot that I'm expecting you home at regular intervals, and if he doesn't comply, I'll report him to his daughter."

Carwyn made a face and Brigid laughed. "You're fighting dirty, Murphy. I'll tell him."

Murphy glanced over his shoulder. "I'm being paged, so I have to go. Keep us updated and call Anne when you get the chance. She misses you."

"I miss her too. Tell Tom and Josie I said hello."

"Not Declan?"

"Fuck no. He knows I can't stand him." She smiled, knowing Declan was probably the one paging Murphy.

On cue, she heard him calling in the background, "I heard that, Brigid!"

She blew the screen a kiss. "Fuck off; I love you all."

The screen and the speaker went blank. Brigid stared at the empty black rectangle, knowing that her life had just inextricably changed. She didn't know what the next chapter would bring, but it would be different. It would be...

An adventure.

Carwyn was standing at the door, holding out his hand. "You ready to go?"

Brigid closed the computer and nodded. "I am."

————

Subscribe to my newsletter for more information about the Elemental Covenant series and the next release, **Martyr's Promise**, coming Fall 2021.

Looking for more to read in the Elemental Universe?

Elemental Mysteries

The four books that started it all!

The explosive international bestseller where history, romance, and the paranormal collide.

A phone call from an old friend sets Giovanni Vecchio back on the path of a mysterious manuscript he's hunted for over five hundred years. He never expected a young student librarian could be the key to unlock its secrets, nor could he have predicted the danger she would attract.

**A Hidden Fire/This Same Earth
The Force of Wind/A Fall of Water**

———

Elemental World

Romance, intrigue, and political suspense set in the Elemental Universe.

Follow your favorite characters from the Elemental Mysteries as they hunt down a deadly vampire drug that threatens the Elemental World.

**Building From Ashes/Waterlocked/Blood and Sand
The Bronze Blade/The Scarlet Deep/A Very Proper
Monster**

A Stone-Kissed Sea/Valley of the Shadow

———

Elemental Legacy
The continuing adventures of Ben Vecchio and Tenzin

What happens when a human raised by vampires teams up with an ancient vampire of impossible power, zero social skills, and an endless fascination with bright, shiny things?
It's very hard to predict.

Prequel novellas:
Shadows and Gold/Imitation and Alchemy
Omens and Artifacts
Novels:
Midnight Labyrinth/Blood Apprentice
Night's Reckoning/Dawn Caravan/The Bone Scroll

ACKNOWLEDGMENTS

I am eternally grateful for the team who keeps me on track and on task. This includes, but is not limited to:

- Genevieve Johnson, assister extraordinaire, who makes me sign all the things and keeps my office navigable
- Amy Cissel, content editor to the stars... and me. Thank you for taking time out of her über-glam life to tell me when I don't need a character to exist or when I've written the word said so often that semantic satiation sets in and all saids said sound like gibberish.
- Bee Whelan, Irish slang beta, who finally settled the whole feck/fuck usage question for me. I am eternally, eternally grateful. As are my Irish readers, no doubt. Relax, you can stop quietly cursing me under your breath now.
- Anne Victory, line editor, comma wrangler, and general grammatical badass. I am so grateful that

you have been willing to work with me for the past many years, despite my inability to figure out that whole lie/lay thing or spell leautenant... liuetenent? Leautenent. No, that's not it.

- Linda, proofreader and woman of mystery. I'd say more about you, but then you'd have to kill me, and neither one of us wants that. I think?

And to all the pros at Damonza.com for their brilliant ideas and willingness to bend over backward for authors who leave things to the last minute, THANK YOU.

———

To all the doctors, nurses, and medical professionals who have worked so hard in the past year to keep our country going, get us vaccinated, hold the hands of the sick and dying, and comfort the grief-stricken while pushing your own needs to the side... we owe you a debt of gratitude that can never be repaid. Bless you and your families. I can write six novels in a year, but I don't have the words to thank you properly.

To the readers who have lifted me up in the past year, thank you. Your encouragement has meant the world to me.

To the tireless delivery drivers who have done their best to keep my family fed while I shamelessly forgot about cooking dinner AGAIN, I hope I tipped you enough. I really tried.

To my dear friends, the Sisterhood, who listen and laugh with me, I am blessed beyond measure to call you my friends. When we can finally head to the bar one Wednesday, the first round is on me.

To my amazing husband and son, I adore you both beyond what is sensible or safe. Thank you for making everything worth it.

———

As always, these acknowledgments are solely my own work and have not been proofread or edited because I like leaving my editors in suspense as to just what inanity I can sneak past them at the end. You can feel free to blame me.

Cheers, EH.

ABOUT THE AUTHOR

ELIZABETH HUNTER is a USA Today and international best-selling author of romance, contemporary fantasy, and paranormal mystery. Based in Central California, she travels extensively to write fantasy fiction exploring world mythologies, history, and the universal bonds of love, friendship, and family. She has published over thirty works of fiction and sold over a million books worldwide. She is the author of the Glimmer Lake series, Love Stories on 7th and Main, the Elemental Legacy series, the Irin Chronicles, the Cambio Springs Mysteries, and other works of fiction.

facebook.com/elizabethhunterwrites
twitter.com/ehunterwrites
bookbub.com/profile/elizabeth-hunter

ALSO BY ELIZABETH HUNTER

The Elemental Covenant

Saint's Passage

Martyr's Promise (Fall, 2021)

The Elemental Mysteries

A Hidden Fire

This Same Earth

The Force of Wind

A Fall of Water

The Stars Afire

The Elemental World

Building From Ashes

Waterlocked

Blood and Sand

The Bronze Blade

The Scarlet Deep

A Very Proper Monster

A Stone-Kissed Sea

Valley of the Shadow

The Elemental Legacy

Shadows and Gold

Imitation and Alchemy

Omens and Artifacts

Obsidian's Edge (anthology)

Midnight Labyrinth

Blood Apprentice

The Devil and the Dancer

Night's Reckoning

Dawn Caravan

The Bone Scroll

(Summer 2021)

The Irin Chronicles

The Scribe

The Singer

The Secret

The Staff and the Blade

The Silent

The Storm

The Seeker

Glimmer Lake

Suddenly Psychic

Semi-Psychic Life

Psychic Dreams

Moonstone Cove

Runaway Fate

Fate Actually

Fate Interrupted (Spring 2021)

The Cambio Springs Series

Long Ride Home

Shifting Dreams

Five Mornings

Desert Bound

Waking Hearts

Linx & Bogie Mysteries

A Ghost in the Glamour

A Bogie in the Boat

Contemporary Romance

The Genius and the Muse

7th and Main

INK

HOOKED

GRIT

Printed in Great Britain
by Amazon

33555198R00158